"We Said No Touching."

Rafiq inched his palm higher. "You said no kissing."

"Rule two, no touching."

Despite Maysa's assertions, he did not bother to lift his hand, and she did not bother to shove it away.

"Yet you have been touching me."

"As a physician."

"And I have reacted as any man reacts to a woman's touch."

"For that reason, I should go now."

Rafiq predicted she would stand and leave, but she remained positioned next to him, both hands still resting lightly on his shoulders. He straightened, bringing their faces close, their gazes connecting immediately. He saw the indecision in her eyes, as well as a spark of need.

And then Maysa did something Rafiq did not expect—she broke her first rule.

Dear Reader,

Each time I settle in front of my computer to begin a book, I always make lots of coffee, hide some kind of candy in my desk drawer and populate a music playlist with selections I believe best capture the mood of the story. Of course, most of those songs are romantic ballads, a no-brainer when you write romance. However, the tunes always vary in terms of genre—from country music to classical—because, simply put, I have extremely eclectic taste in music, as well as an affinity for all things chocolate.

I didn't veer from my usual routine when I began *One Night with the Sheikh.* After I'd decided where I wanted the story to go, I immediately went to work finding specific tunes that I felt would be inspirational. I chose several songs by various performers, including Journey, Don Henley and New Age artist Constance Demby, by virtue of her hauntingly beautiful instrumentals. But I have to admit, the two standouts on the list are "One of These Nights" by the Eagles and "Desert Rose" by Sting. If you're curious to know exactly what was filtering through my headphones during the love scenes, chances are it was one of these two songs.

When King Rafiq Mehdi and Dr. Maysa Barad are anywhere near each other, you can bet there will be a high level of chemistry, and they deserve background music to match. After all, they've never forgotten that one incredible night they spent together years ago. But sometimes one night just isn't quite enough—even if it is forbidden.

Hope you enjoy the beautiful music Rafiq and Maysa make together!

Kristi

KRISTI GOLD

ONE NIGHT WITH THE SHEIKH

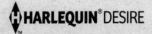

Recycling programs
for this product may
not exist in your area.

ISBN-13: 978-0-373-73257-9

ONE NIGHT WITH THE SHEIKH

Printed in U.S.A.

KRISTI GOLD

has a fondness for beaches, baseball and bridal reality shows. She firmly believes that love has remarkable, healing powers and feels very fortunate to be able to weave stories of love and commitment. As a bestselling author, a National Readers' Choice Award winner and a Romance Writers of America three-time RITA® Award finalist, Kristi has learned that although accolades are wonderful, the most cherished rewards come from networking with readers. She can be reached through her website at www.kristigold.com or through Facebook.

To my beautiful daughter, Kendall.
One of the best Athletic Trainers in the business,
one of my biggest fans,
and one of my major sources for chocolate.

One

King Rafiq ibn Fayiz Mehdi possessed keen intelligence, vast power and infinite riches. Yet none had aided him in preventing a devastating tragedy—a tragedy for which he had been partially responsible.

As the sun began to set, he stood on the palace's rooftop veranda and peered at the panorama stretched out before him. The diverse terrain he once revered now seemed ominous, inviting disturbing recollections that cut into his composure like a well-honed blade.

A dark, winding road at midnight. Silence and dread. Flashing lights illuminating the bottom of a cliff. The twisted metal wreckage…

"If you believe you'll move mountains by staring at them, I assure you it will not work."

At the sound of the familiar voice, Rafiq glanced back to see his brother standing only a few steps behind him. "Why are you here?"

Zain claimed the space beside Rafiq and leaned back against the stone wall. "Is that how you greet the man who so generously handed you the keys to the kingdom over a year ago?"

The same man who had abdicated the throne for the sake of love, an emotion Rafiq had never quite embraced. "My apologies, brother. I was not expecting you for another month."

"Since I completed my initial preparation for the water conservation project, I felt the timing was right for my return."

Under normal circumstances, he would appreciate Zain's company. Lately he preferred solitude. "Did you travel alone?"

"Of course not," Zain said in an irritable tone. "I do not travel without my family unless absolutely necessary."

Rafiq had never believed he would hear his womanizing brother utter those words. "Then Madison is with you?"

"Yes, and my children. I've been anxious for you to finally meet your niece and nephew."

Rafiq did not share in Zain's enthusiasm. Being in the presence of two infants would only serve to remind him of what he had lost. "Where are they now?"

"Madison and Elena are tending to them."

At least he could temporarily avoid the painful introduction. "I am glad you have finally returned Elena to her rightful place. The household does not run well without her."

"So I have heard," Zain said. "I have also heard you are in danger of causing an uprising among the palace staff if you continue to terrorize them."

Rafiq admittedly had trouble maintaining calm in recent days, but he did not care for the exaggerated accusation. "I have not terrorized the staff. I have only corrected them when necessary."

"It's my understanding you have found it necessary to *correct* them on a daily basis, brother. I've also learned you have not been cooperative with the council."

Rafiq began to question the real reason behind Zain's surprise appearance. "Have you been speaking with our younger brother?"

Zain's gaze faltered. "I have been in touch with Adan on occasion."

His anger began to build. "And you have clearly been discussing me."

"He only mentioned you've been having a difficult time since Rima's death."

Rafiq's suspicions had been confirmed—Zain had arrived early to play nursemaid. "Despite what you and Adan might believe, I do not need a keeper."

Zain leaned forward, his expression suddenly somber. "We both understand how devastating it must be to lose your wife and your unborn child—"

"How could you understand?" No one would ever understand the constant guilt and regret unless they had experienced it. "You have a wife and two healthy children."

"As I was saying," Zain continued, "it's understandable that you are still harboring a good measure of anger, particularly with so many unanswered questions about the accident. However, your attitude is proving disruptive. Perhaps you should consider taking a sabbatical."

Impossible and unnecessary. "And who would run the country in my stead?"

"I would," Zain said. "After all, I prepared many years to assume that responsibility before I gave up the position. Adan is willing to assist me."

Rafiq released a cynical laugh. "First, Adan has no interest in governing Bajul. He's only interested in flying planes and seducing women. As far as you are concerned, our people have not forgotten you abandoned them for a second time."

Barely contained fury called out from Zain's narrowed eyes. "I still have an abiding love for this country, and I am quite capable of seeing that it runs smoothly, as I promised before I returned with Madison to the States. Do not forget, I alone developed the water conservation plan that will secure Bajul's future. And I have earned the council's support."

Rafiq recognized he had been wrong to criticize Zain. "My apologies. I do appreciate your support, but I assure you I do not need a sabbatical."

"A sabbatical would allow you to assess your feelings about the situation."

Rafiq was growing weary of the interference. "My *feelings* are not significant. My duties to Bajul are of the utmost importance."

"Yet your emotional upheaval has understandably begun to affect your leadership. Grieving requires time, Rafiq. You have not allowed yourself enough for that."

He had grieved more than anyone would know. "It has been six months. Life must continue as planned."

Zain whisked a hand through his dark hair. "Plans go awry, brother, and life sometimes comes to a standstill. You have suffered a great loss and if you choose not to acknowledge that, you will only suffer more."

He could no longer suffer through this conversation. "I prefer not to discuss it further, so if you will excuse me—"

The sound of footfalls silenced Rafiq and drew his attention to Zain's blonde American bride walking toward them, a round-faced, dark-haired infant propped on one hip. He immediately noticed the happiness reflected in his sister-in-law's face and the obvious adoration in her blue eyes when she met Zain's gaze. "I have a baby girl who insists on being with her daddy."

Zain presented a warm smile. "And her father is more than happy to accommodate her."

After Madison handed the infant to Zain, she drew Rafiq into an embrace. "It's good to see you, my dear brother-in-law."

"And you, Madison," he said. "You are looking well, as usual. I would never have known you had given birth." Ironically, only a few days after he had buried his wife.

She pushed her somewhat disheveled hair back and blushed. "Thank you. Elena told me to tell you that she'll see you as soon as she has Joseph in bed. She seems to be able to calm our son better than anyone, but then after raising the Mehdi boys, she's had quite a bit of experience."

Zain moved closer to Rafiq and regarded his child. "Cala, this is your uncle Rafiq. And yes, we do favor each other, except for that goatee, but I am much more handsome."

Rafiq experienced sheer sadness at the sound of his mother's name that his brother had given his daughter.

The mother he had barely known yet still revered. "She is a beautiful child, Zain. Congratulations."

"Do you wish to hold your niece?" Zain asked.

If he dared, he risked destroying the emotional fortress he had built for protection. "Perhaps later. At the moment I have some documents to review." He leaned and kissed Madison's cheek. "You have honored my brother by giving him the greatest of gifts. For that, I am grateful."

Needing to escape, Rafiq strode across the veranda, only to be halted by Zain, who handed the child back to Madison and followed him to the door. "Wait, Rafiq."

He reluctantly faced his brother again. "What is it now?"

Zain rested a hand on Rafiq's shoulder. "I understand why it would be difficult to discuss anything involving emotional issues with your siblings. For that reason, I believe you should seek out a friend who understands you better than most."

He could only recall one soul who would currently meet that requirement, and they had not interacted as friends in quite some time. "If you are referring to Shamil Barad, he is away while the resort is being renovated."

"I am referring to his sister, Maysa."

The name sent a spear of regret through Rafiq's heart, and a rush of memories into his mind. He recalled the way her long, dark hair cascaded down her back and fell below her waist. The deep creases in her cheeks that framed her beautiful smile. He remembered the way she had looked that long-ago night when they had made love—their greatest mistake. He also remembered the pain in her brown eyes the day he had told her they could never be together. "I have not spoken with Maysa at length in many years. She severed all ties when—"

"You chose Rima Acar over her?"

He did not care to defend the decision, but he would. "I was not consulted when the agreement between our fathers was made."

Zain rubbed his shaded jaw. "Ah, yes. I believe Sheikh Acar trumped Maysa's father's offer during the bridal bartering. I also recall that you did nothing to plead your case. You never attempted to convince either party that you belonged with Maysa."

And he had regretted that decision more than once. "In accordance with tradition, it was not within my power to do so."

Zain's expression turned to stone. "A tradition that forced me to choose between my royal duty and my wife. An antiquated custom that has done nothing but lead to your misery, and Maysa's, as well. The choice the sultan made for Maysa resulted in divorce and nearly ruined her, and you were anything but happy with your queen."

Anger as hot as a firebrand shot through Rafiq. "You know nothing about my relationship with Rima."

"I know what I witnessed when I saw the two of you together." Zain studied him for a long moment. "Were you happy, Rafiq? Was Rima happy?"

He could not answer truthfully without confirming Zain's conjecture. "I cared a great deal for Rima. We were friends long before we wed. Her death has been difficult for me, whether you choose to believe that or not."

"My apologies for sounding insensitive," Zain said.

"As I told you earlier, it's very apparent you are in great turmoil, which brings me back to my suggestion you talk with Maysa. She will understand."

Perhaps so, but other issues still existed. "Even if she agreed to see me, which I suspect she will not, any liaison with Maysa would not be considered acceptable. She is divorced and I have been widowed for only a brief time."

Zain's frustration came out in a scowl. "First of all, I am only suggesting you speak with her, not wed her. Second, if you are concerned that someone will assume an affair, then steal away in the night to prevent detection. It has always worked to my advantage. Should you need assistance, I will be glad to make the arrangements."

He had no doubt Zain could. His brother had made covert disappearance an art form. "I do not need your assistance, nor do I plan to see Maysa."

"Do not dismiss it completely, Rafiq. She could be the one person to see you through this difficult phase."

At one time, that would have held true. Maysa had known him better than any living soul, understood him better, and she had been a welcome source of support during their formative years. She had also been his greatest weakness, and he had been her greatest disappointment.

For that reason, he should stay away from her. Yet as he left his brother's company and returned to his quarters, alone with his continuing guilt, he began to wonder if perhaps Zain might be right. Reconnecting with Maysa again, if only for a brief time, could very well be worth the risks.

* * *

As the village's primary physician, Maysa Barad answered the midnight summons expecting a messenger requesting she tend to an ailing child or a mother in labor. She did not expect to find Rafiq Mehdi, the recently crowned—and newly widowed—King of Bajul. Her childhood friend. Her first love. Her first lover.

The changes in Rafiq were somewhat apparent, but subtle. He was still tall and lean. Still as incredibly handsome as he'd always been, despite that he now chose to wear a neatly trimmed goatee framing his sensual mouth. His eyes and hair were still as dark, much the same as hers, yet maturity had lent him an even greater aura of power. A power that had crushed her resolve on more than one occasion many years before.

She could not remember the last time he had called on her. She couldn't imagine why he was here now, but she intended to find out. "Good evening, Your Majesty. To what do I owe this pleasure?"

"I need to speak with you."

His serious tone and intense gaze prompted Maysa to press the panic button. "Are you ill?"

"No. I will explain why I am here as soon as we are in a private setting."

Maysa glanced around him to see a black car parked in the portico, and surprisingly not one of the requisite sentries. "Where are your guards?"

"At the palace. Only select members of my staff know I am here."

Being completely alone with him somewhat concerned Maysa. She considered asking him to return in the morning, when she was appropriately dressed, well rested and better prepared. However, he was still the king and his wish would have to be her command, an all too familiar concept. During their youth, she would have done anything he asked of her. One fateful night, she had.

Despite all the concerns racing through her mind, and the threat to her composure, she opened the door wide to allow him entry. "I suppose you may come in for a while."

After Rafiq stepped into the foyer, Maysa closed and locked the door, then faced him to find his dark, pensive gaze leveled on hers. "I sincerely appreciate your willingness to see me at this hour," he said without a hint of familiarity.

She sincerely questioned the wisdom in allowing him in her home. "You are welcome. Follow me."

Maysa led him down the corridor and paused when one of the staff appeared from around the corner. She waved the befuddled woman away and continued past the myriad rooms comprising the expansive house belonging to her father, and on loan to her. The same house where she'd gone from teenager to woman in her childhood bed, courtesy of the man walking behind her.

Once they reached her private living area, she shut the door and gestured toward the settee. "Feel free to be seated."

"I prefer to stand," he said as he began to pace the room like a caged tiger, his hands firmly planted in the pockets of his black slacks.

Maysa dropped down onto the sofa, curled her legs beneath her and adjusted the aqua caftan to where it covered her bare feet. She chose to continue to speak in English, should one of the staff decide to eavesdrop. "What can I do for you, Rafiq?"

He stopped to stare out the window overlooking the mountains. "I could not sleep. I've had difficulty sleeping since…"

"The accident," she said when his words trailed away. The mysterious, single-car accident that had claimed the queen's life six months ago. "Insomnia and restlessness are understandable. Rima's death was tragic and unexpected. If you would like me to prescribe a sleep aid, I would certainly be willing to do that."

He turned toward her, some unnamed emotion in his near-black eyes. "I do not wish a pill, Maysa. I wish to go back to that night and find a way to prevent my wife's death. I want to find some peace."

His feelings for his queen apparently were much deeper than Maysa had realized. "It takes time to recover from losing someone you cared about, Rafiq."

"It has been six months," he said. "And I did not care enough, which directly contributed to her demise."

Evidently she had made an erroneous assumption. It seemed Rafiq's marriage to Rima Acar had been little more than a long-standing agreement between their patriarchs. Yet she didn't understand why he blamed himself for her death. "You weren't driving the car, Rafiq."

He crossed the room and joined her on the opposite end of the small settee. "But I did drive her away that night."

She wasn't certain she wanted to hear the details, but since he'd decided to take her into his confidence for the first time in years, she chose to listen. "Did you argue before she left?"

He lowered his head and streaked his palms over his face, as if to erase the bitter memories. "Yes, immediately after she informed me she was with child."

Rima's pregnancy had been kept from the press, but the revelation came as no surprise to Maysa. Unbeknownst to the king, the queen had come to her for confirmation instead of consulting the palace physician, though she never quite understood why. Rima had always been aware of Maysa's close relationship with Rafiq, at times pitting them as rivals. "Were you not happy to hear the news?"

"I was pleased to know I would have an heir. She was not at all pleased to be having my child."

Maysa had witnessed Rima's distress when she'd delivered the results, but she had attributed that to slight shock. "She told you that?"

He released a rough sigh. "Not in so many words, but I sensed her unhappiness. When I questioned her at length, she did not deny it. She disappeared some time later without my knowledge."

Maysa experienced a measure of satisfaction that he'd chosen to release his burden and a good deal of guilt over what she'd chosen to withhold from him. She suspected she knew where the queen had been before the accident, though she had no solid proof. "Do you know where she might have been going when she left?"

His expression remained somber. "No, and I most likely will never know. I do know if I had been kinder to her, then perhaps she would not have felt the need to leave."

She offered him the only advice she could give him at the moment. Advice she had been forced to follow since the day he'd told her he would be marrying another, shattering her dreams of a future with him. "Rafiq, you can spend a lifetime wondering what might have been, or you can move on with your life."

"I told Zain only hours ago that I intended to proceed with my life," he said. "I did not admit the difficulty in that. To him, or until recently, myself."

"It would be nice if your brother were here during this trying time."

Rafiq kept his gaze trained on the floor. "He arrived in Bajul today with Madison and their children."

She realized having the children around could be the basis for his lack of enthusiasm and distress. "That must be very difficult for you."

He finally looked at her. "Why would you believe I would not welcome my brother's family?"

She laid a hand on his arm. "Of course you would, but being in the presence of two infants might remind you of your recent loss."

"I can handle that, but I cannot abide Zain's advice. He is convinced I need a sabbatical."

"Perhaps he is right. Time away would aid in the healing process."

He frowned. "He is wrong. I only need time to adjust. I can accomplish that and still tend to my duties."

As far as she was concerned, he was overestimating his strength. "Does Zain know you're here?"

"Yes. He insisted I talk with you."

Maysa's hopes had been dashed once more. "I thought perhaps you came on your own."

"I would never have thought to bother you," he said.

"It's no bother, Rafiq. I considered visiting you after the funeral, but I wasn't at all certain I would be welcome."

He looked at her somberly, sincerely. "You will always be welcome in my world, Maysa."

The memory hit her full force then. The memory of a time when he'd spoken those same words to her.

No matter what the future holds, you will always be welcome in my world, habibti....

Yet she had not been welcome at all. After his marriage contract had been finalized, they had been expressly forbidden to see each other, yet they had continued to meet in secret. Those clandestine trysts had only fueled the fire between them until one night, they had made love the first—and the last—time.

Maysa wondered if Rafiq remembered. She wondered if he recalled those remarkable moments, or if he had pushed them out of his thoughts. She wondered why she had been such a fool to believe he would have changed his mind about marrying Rima.

She rose to her feet and crossed the room to pour a glass of water from a pitcher set out on a side table. She kept her back to Rafiq as she took a few sips, and swallowed hard when she heard approaching footsteps.

"Have I said something to upset you, Maysa?"

His presence upset her. Her feelings for him upset her. She set the glass on the table and turned to him. "Why are you really here, Rafiq? Why have you come to me after all these years?"

His expression reflected confusion. "You are the one person I have always turned to for solace."

"Not always," she said. "We've been virtual strangers for well over a decade."

His expression implied building anger. "You were the one who left Bajul for the States, Maysa. I have always been here."

"I had no choice after I divorced Boutros."

"A man you should have never wed."

A heartless, angry sultan who had almost stolen her sense of self-worth and security. Almost. "As it was with you and Rima, my marriage was no more than an edict from my father."

Rafiq inclined his head and studied her. "Why did you risk your name and reputation to divorce him?"

She did not dare tell him the entire truth. "He refused to allow me to pursue my profession. I refused to allow him to tell me how to live my life."

He looked as if he could see right through her. "That is the only reason?"

"Isn't that enough? And what other reason would there be?"

Now he appeared cynical. "Everyone is quite aware of Boutros Kassab's reputation for suspect business arrangements and questionable connections."

She would simply allow him to believe that rather than reveal the harsh reality—Boutros was a sadistic, uncaring lecher. "I was eighteen when we married, Rafiq. I had no involvement in his business dealings. I was only required to play the dutiful wife."

He raised a brow. "In his bed?"

She hesitated slightly. "Do you wish me to lie and say no?"

"He is thirty years your senior. I hoped you would say he had little interest in anything of a carnal nature due to an inability to perform."

Many nights she had wished that had only been the case, but it had not. "Boutros is a man, and men rarely lose interest in sex, no matter what their age."

"Did he satisfy you, Maysa?"

She was momentarily stunned. "That is none of your concern."

He streamed a fingertip down her cheek. "I am only curious if he knew how to please you. If he learned, as I did, how to make you tremble with need."

She circled her arms around her middle as if that might afford her protection from his magnetic pull. From the memories. "Did Rima satisfy you, Rafiq? Or did you simply go to her for the sake of producing an heir?" The moment the words left her mouth, she silently cursed her thoughtlessness.

Rafiq reacted by turning away, crossing the room and moving to the window to stare at the mountains once more. She approached him slowly and rested a palm on his shoulder. "I am so sorry, Rafiq. I did not mean to be so unkind. I know how much you are hurting over the loss of your child. I also know that you did care very much for your wife, and you were a good husband to her. You would never ignore her needs."

"And in doing so, I was forced to disregard what I needed most."

"And that was?"

"You."

Without warning, Rafiq spun around and crushed Maysa against him. He claimed her mouth with a vengeance, with a touch of desperation. And as she always had, she willingly accepted the kiss.

She hated that he could so easily mold her into a willing, wanton woman, but not quite enough to stop him. She despised herself for wanting to give in to the ever-present desire. To do so could lead to undeniable pleasure, and quite possibly disaster. He didn't necessarily want her. He only wanted comfort wherever available, as it had been all those years ago. And that made her furious enough to recapture her common sense.

With all the strength she could muster, Maysa moved back, putting some much-needed distance between them. "How many women were there after me and prior to your marriage to Rima?"

Confusion crossed over his expression. "Why does that matter?"

"Perhaps you could call on one of them to provide the escape you so obviously need."

His handsome features turned to stone. "You truly believe that is all you mean to me?"

She folded her arms beneath her breasts. "Yes, I do. You're only seeking a temporary diversion, and after you receive it, you will be gone again."

"I seek the company of someone I trust. Someone I have always cared about."

"If you truly cared about me, you would not have kissed me."

"Perhaps the kiss was a mistake," he said. "Perhaps I should not have come here."

She released a disparaging laugh. "You're right. It was a mistake. Someone could find out, and that would not go over well with the elders. I am a scorned woman, remember? A divorcée and to some, the equivalent of a harlot. And let us not forget you are the almighty king."

"You have never been a harlot in my eyes," he said adamantly. "And at times I wish to forget I am the king."

The sudden dejection in his tone tugged at Maysa's heartstrings. "It sounds as if you *could* use a sabbatical."

"I have nowhere to go where I would be left alone." He fixed his gaze firmly on hers as his lips curled into the familiar teasing smile. The one that had always crushed her determination. "Unless, of course, you would be willing to open your home to me. I would keep to myself. You would not know I am here."

She would know he was there every moment of the day, whether in his presence or not. "I question the wisdom in that plan."

He took her hands into his. "I only wish for time away from my responsibilities, and to become reacquainted with a friend."

How very easy it would be to agree to his request, but… "You have no wish to become reacquainted in bed?"

"I would never ask anything of you that you are not willing to give."

That alone presented a problem—she could find herself willing to give him everything, receiving nothing in return aside from nights of pleasure and more good memories to temporarily overcome the bad. He could also break her heart once more.

Maysa tugged out of his grasp and strolled around the room, all the while weighing the pros and cons. Then something suddenly occurred to her. She could use his presence to her advantage. She could finally show him that improvements to health care for the poor should be paramount during his reign. She could introduce him to exactly what his people endured in the face of illness. And she would do so while keeping her wits about her.

After all, the guest wing was far removed from her private suites, allowing them physical distance. Aside from that, she was a strong, independent woman. She had superb skills honed at the best medical facilities in the United States. She had survived and divorced a known tyrant. She could handle a king—or so she hoped.

On that thought, she faced Rafiq again, lifted her chin, and centered her gaze on his. "All right. You may stay." When he began to speak, she held up a finger to silence him. "As long as you abide by my rules."

He sent her a suspicious look. "What would these rules entail?"

"I prefer to reserve the details for later." When she actually knew what they were.

"All right," he said. "Is there anything else you require of me tonight?"

One response vaulted into her brain. An inappropriate response that she shoved aside. "Not at this time."

Rafiq regarded his watch before bringing his attention back to her. "I must return to the palace now. We shall continue this discussion when I arrive tomorrow to begin my respite."

Tomorrow? "I thought perhaps you would need more time to make arrangements." Or to change his mind.

"I have complete control over when I stay or when I leave the palace. After all, I am—"

"The king. I know." All too well. "I'll see you out."

They walked side by side to the door where Rafiq paused and regarded her earnestly. "I am forever in your debt, Maysa, and I assure you I will give you no cause to distrust my motives."

That remained to be seen. "I'm pleased to know that. And I reserve the right to add conditions should your motives come into question."

"I will strive to win back your trust. The way you once trusted me before our lives intruded on our relationship."

Maysa wanted to believe him. More important, she wanted not to be so drawn to him. Wanted not to feel so lost when he looked at her as he looked at her now—with a heated gaze that traveled from her forehead to her mouth.

They stood for a few long moments, face-to-face, the tension as thick as the mountain mist. Maysa recognized that it would only take a slight move toward him before they found themselves lips to lips. Body to body.

She finally cleared her throat and stepped back before her resolve shattered. "Have a good night, King Mehdi. I will see you tomorrow."

"I will be here before day's end, Dr. Barad."

The formality surprised Maysa and sounded false to her ears. Yet if that formality kept her grounded, she would avoid calling him by his given name. Avoid touching him altogether. Avoid any circumstance that could lead to risks neither could afford to take. But when he leaned and brushed a soft kiss across her cheek, and presented a soft, sensual smile, she worried danger could lurk around every corner when he returned to her home.

After Rafiq opened the door and strode out of the house toward the awaiting car, Maysa considered the first rule. An important rule that could save her from herself. "Rafiq," she called before he could settle into the seat. "I have one more thing to say before you go."

He turned with a wary look on his face. "You have reconsidered?"

She hadn't, though she probably should. "No. I have thought of one rule that we both must follow."

"And that is?"

"There will be no more kisses."

He sent her a knowing smile before he slid into the car. And as Maysa watched the taillights disappear, she worried that King Rafiq Mehdi could convince her to break all the rules.

Two

No more kisses...

As Rafiq sat alone in his office, attempting to tie up loose ends, kissing Maysa remained foremost on his mind. Making love to her again did, as well. He could no more resist the fantasies than he could pick up the palace with his bare hands and move it down the mountainside.

"Have you mentally vacated the premises, brother?"

Rafiq glanced up from his desk to discover his youngest sibling standing before him, wearing his usual standard beige flight suit and mocking smile. "I am preoccupied by my duty."

"Too preoccupied to speak with me, your most loyal supporter?"

Adan rarely supported anyone aside from himself. "Unless you have something important to say, you may return later."

"I do have something of great importance to tell you," Adan said as he claimed the opposing chair.

Frustrated over the intrusion, Rafiq tossed his pen aside and leaned back in his seat. "You have found yet another aircraft you are determined to add to our fleet."

"No. I came to deliver a message."

"From whom?"

"Maysa Barad." Adan's grin widened, as if privy to a secret. "She requests that you arrive before 6:00 p.m., and that you limit your guards if at all possible."

He could only imagine where his brother's thoughts had turned. "Duly noted. You may leave now."

"Not until you explain why you are visiting Maysa, and why she would ask that you not bring along too many guards. Either she feels she does not pose a threat, or she wishes to make certain she has your undivided attention."

"What business I have with Maysa is not your concern."

"Perhaps, but I am curious."

Rafiq resisted telling his brother what he could do with his curiosity, and his British accent. "If you must know, Maysa has agreed to allow me to take a brief respite in her home."

Adan rubbed his chin. "I see. Will you be spending this respite in her bed?"

He was not at all surprised over the assumption, but he *was* angered by it. "Rest assured, I will not be attempting to bed her." Though preventing that possibility would prove to be a great challenge.

Adan released a cynical laugh. "Ah, that is where we differ. I for one would give up flying before I would not take advantage of being alone with a beautiful woman in close confines. And you should consider doing the same."

He felt the need to explain his resistance, whether Adan deserved an explanation or not. "First, I have only been widowed a short while—"

"To a woman you did not love."

"A woman I had known for quite some time before she became my wife. No matter what you believe, I did care for Rima."

"Yet not as much as you've always cared for Maysa."

His patience was beginning to grow thin, frayed in part by the truth. "Maysa is only a friend who has agreed to accommodate my needs."

"Which needs would those be, brother?" Adan asked.

"My intentions are honorable." Though his thoughts and actions the previous evening had not been at all honorable.

"How honorable will you be while spending time with a friend who at one time fancied herself in love with you?"

He could not argue that point. "What Maysa and I shared in the past had more to do with camaraderie than with love."

"Teenage lust, you mean. And that lust could quite possibly carry over into adulthood."

He had spent most of the night considering it. "I am older and wiser. I have learned to maintain self-control."

Adan presented a skeptic's smile. "You are a Mehdi male, Rafiq, and self-control can and will escape you in the presence of a woman you have always desired. You are not made of steel."

Rafiq folded his hands atop the desk and glared at his brother. "Do not project your lack of restraint on me. I have not made bedding women my favorite pastime."

"I have not had as many women as you might believe," Adan said. "And although you have practiced more discretion, I suspect you were not celibate during the time between your agreement to marry Rima and when you finally did wed her."

That fact was not up for debate. "If you are finished delving into my private life, you may take your leave immediately."

"Actually, I'm not quite finished. Did it disturb you that Rima was not a virgin when you wed her?"

Adan's audacity made Rafiq's blood boil. "Why would you assume this?"

"Are you denying it?"

Unfortunately, he could not. Yet he did question how Adan would know something so personal about Rima. He was tempted to ask, but he in turn feared the answer. "This topic is not up for discussion."

"I only wanted to point out that Rima was not destined for sainthood," Adan said. "Neither are you. In fact, you're human, and a man with needs."

The reason behind his brother's insinuation finally dawned on Rafiq. "If you are worried I will bring scandal upon the Mehdi name by sleeping with Maysa, I assure you that will not happen. And if you are also hoping that I will abandon my duty and pass the crown to you, as Zain did with me, you may set those wishes aside immediately."

Adan's expression turned suddenly serious. "I have never possessed any desire to be king, Rafiq. And as far as your relationship with Maysa is concerned, I am an advocate for letting nature take its course. If you and Maysa find you cannot resist each other, then don't. You certainly have my blessing."

Adan had failed to weigh the most important fact. If Rafiq took Maysa as his lover again, the liaison could only be temporary since he would be expected to choose a suitable queen. The thought of being with another woman aside from Maysa was unthinkable. The thought of wounding her again, unimaginable. Yet he could very well head down that path if he acted on impulse.

For that reason, perhaps he should consider canceling their arrangement. Perhaps it would be best if he found another location for his sabbatical. "I will take your counsel under advisement. Now if you do not mind, I have work to complete."

"So much work, *il mio bel ragazzo,* that you cannot give your former governess a few moments?"

Rafiq turned his attention from Adan to Elena Battelli, who now stood at the doorway, a dark-haired infant balanced on her hip. Her silver hair contrasted with her topaz eyes that at times hinted at mischief, and other times reflected wisdom. She had been the Mehdi sons' surrogate matriarch since their mother's death, and always a welcome presence. She had also been free with her opinions, and he expected no less from her now.

Rafiq came to his feet, rounded the desk and accepted her embrace. "I am glad to see you have returned home, Elena. You are looking quite well."

"You are looking tired, *cara,*" she said as she handed the baby off to an overtly surprised Adan. "Take your niece to her father and allow me some time alone with your brother."

Rising from the chair, Adan gripped the child awkwardly and looked as if he had consumed something unpalatable. "What if she begins to cry on the way?"

Elena frowned. "She would not be the first female you've made cry, so I suggest you hurry."

As soon as Adan left with the squirming infant, Rafiq seated himself behind the desk while Elena claimed the chair opposite his. She studied him for a long moment before she spoke. "What is this I hear about you spending time with Dr. Barad?"

He should not be surprised Elena would join his brothers by presenting her thoughts on the matter. Yet her opinion had always mattered most. He also suspected she would side with Zain. "It is not what you might believe it to be."

"I believe, *cara mia,* it is a good idea."

He had not predicted that reaction. "I am beginning to question the wisdom in the plan."

"Because you fear what others might think?"

Because he feared his possible absence of strength in Maysa's presence. "I do not wish to add undue stress to her life."

Elena waved a hand in dismissal. "Maysa is well equipped to handle stress, Rafiq, and perhaps even better equipped to handle you."

He was taken aback by her assertions. "What are you saying?"

"I am saying she knows you very well." Elena laid a palm on his hand. "She has always been your touchstone, and I believe you need that right now, more than you need the throne. And if you are concerned that you might succumb to inadvisable urges, I trust you to be the honorable man you have always been."

If only he could trust himself. "Then you sincerely believe I should continue with my plans?"

"Yes, I do." She rose with the grace of a gazelle. "Do not forget what I've taught you. *Chi trova un amico trova un tesoro.*"

He who finds a friend, finds a treasure.

As Elena started toward the door, she sent Rafiq a smile over one shoulder. "Maysa is your treasure, *cara.* Do not squander that gift."

Maysa had begun to believe Rafiq had changed his mind. When the doorbell chimed, she hurried down the hall to answer the summons but then slowed her steps so as not to seem too anxious, though she was. Yet when she opened the door, the bearded man on the threshold happened to be her brother, not the king. "What are you doing here, Shamil?"

"I expected a more enthusiastic greeting, considering my recent absence," he said as he breezed past her and entered without an invitation.

"My apologies," she said as she faced him in the foyer. "I'm just surprised to see you."

"Were you expecting someone else?"

She chose to withhold the truth and settled for a change in subject. "Are the resort's renovations complete?"

"No, and that is why I am here now," he said. "I will be returning to Yemen tonight, and I would respectfully request you supervise the workers from time to time in my stead."

The request did not surprise her in the least. Shamil

always seemed to have an ulterior motive when he bothered to call on her. He had protested the loudest over her divorce, and had chastised her at every turn—until he wanted something. "I have a medical practice that requires my attention, Shamil. I do not have time to oversee a project that you took on."

"Need I remind you the resort is partially your responsibility?"

She could not believe his audacity. "Our father handed the keys to the resort to you, not me."

"And he handed this house to you," he said as he made a sweeping gesture over the area. "All because he is a generous and forgiving man. I would be remiss if I did not mention that he initially arranged for the hotel's restoration. I am certain it would please him if he knew you were assisting me. He would not be pleased if he learned you refused to provide that assistance."

Maysa was beyond trying to please her father, and immune to Shamil's veiled threats. "I can only promise that I will stop by once a week, provided I find the time."

"Twice a week, or perhaps three times, would be preferable."

She would agree to most anything if it encouraged her sibling's speedy departure. "I will try. Is that all you wish from me?"

"For the moment. I will notify the staff you will be periodically stopping by."

"All right."

When Maysa moved toward the door and yanked it open, she heard the sound of a car pulling into the portico.

"What is *he* doing here?" Shamil asked, both his tone and expression balanced on the brink of contempt.

She ventured a backward glance to see Rafiq emerging from the sedan with a heavily armed guard standing nearby. "First of all, he is the king, and he is allowed to go anywhere he pleases. Second, he is a friend, and at one time, your best friend."

"He no longer holds that distinction."

Maysa's attempt to question her brother further was thwarted when Rafiq joined them at the doorstep.

Rafiq smiled at Maysa and briefly nodded at Shamil. *"As-salam alaikum."*

"Wa alaikum as-salam," Shamil replied in a voice that heralded indifference along with a touch of disdain. "Have you forgotten the way to the palace, Sayyed?"

"Not at all," Rafiq replied. "I am here by invitation."

Shamil sent Maysa a lethal look before returning his attention to Rafiq. "If you are here to discuss health care issues with my sister, it would be appropriate to do so in a less private setting."

Concerned over her brother's caustic demeanor, Maysa stepped aside to allow Rafiq entry. "The staff will show you to your quarters, Your Highness."

"As you wish," he said without offering Shamil even a passing glance.

She sensed her brother's glare before she actually contacted it. She turned and gave him a glare of her own. "How dare you be so ill-mannered."

"How dare you invite him into our father's house."

"Our father has always had close ties to the Mehdi family," Maysa said. "He would not be opposed to having a member as a houseguest, particularly if that member happens to be the sovereign ruler of Bajul. A king who is in need of a respite, which is why he will be staying here for a time."

"Our father would be opposed to you becoming the king's mistress."

Her fury simmered just below the surface of her feigned calm. "You have no right to speak to me this way, nor do you have any reason to hate Rafiq. Or do you still envy his marriage to Rima?"

He looked as if he might strike the wall, or worse, his sister. "Rima meant nothing to Rafiq," he growled. "He did not deserve her."

Clearly Shamil had not moved beyond the past, or his desire for a woman he could never have. But hadn't she been guilty of the same with Rafiq? No. She had moved on, and would continue to do so. "How would you know what privately transpired between the king and queen, Shamil?"

"She deserved far more care and concern than Rafiq afforded her. She deserved the chance to live, and he stole that chance from her."

"Rafiq had no hand in Rima's death."

"You would not agree if you had seen her that night."

Maysa felt as if they might be hurling toward the truth of what had transpired that evening. What she herself had witnessed. "Perhaps I did see her after all."

That seemed to momentarily douse Shamil's wrath. "Where would you have seen her?"

"I drove to the resort earlier that evening and when I saw you embracing a woman on the veranda, I immediately left. Am I correct to assume that woman was Rima?" When he failed to respond, she added, "Shamil, was it Rima?"

His gaze faltered. "She was there for a brief time."

"And how many times before that?"

"That is not your concern."

Oh, but it was. "Were the two of you having an affair?"

"Enough!"

She'd obviously struck a nerve encased in the truth. "And Rafiq knew nothing about your liaison with his wife."

"Rafiq knew nothing about Rima's life because he chose not to know." He sent her a steely look. "And he will never know. Is that understood?"

One more threat among many. "He has a right to know what happened in the minutes leading up to her death."

"He gave up all rights to that knowledge when he discarded her feelings and deprived her of freedom. And if you utter one word of this conversation to the king, then I will see to it you are removed from this house and I will make certain your reputation is ruined beyond repair."

She clung tightly to the last thread of civility. "You do not have that much power, Shamil. You never have. I can find another place to live, and the villagers respect me not only as their doctor, but as a person. They care not about my past."

He narrowed his eyes and stared at her. "Will they be so accepting if they learn their doctor is also the king's *sharmuta?*"

She pointed a shaky finger at the SUV parked at the end of the drive. "Leave now and do not return unless you arrive with an apology."

He released a bitter laugh. "Oh, I will return, yet I

will not rescind what I have said. If you reveal any details to Rafiq, there will be consequences."

With that, he rushed to the waiting SUV and drove away, leaving Maysa standing on the threshold, worrying over how she would tell Rafiq about his wife's whereabouts that fateful evening. *If* she decided to tell him.

Should she confess, the outcome would still be the same. Rima would still be gone, her secrets following her to the grave. Shamil would be bent on ruining Maysa's life if she told Rafiq the details. She had very limited loyalty to Shamil, but she possessed enough common sense not to risk losing everything she had worked so hard to build. Yet the thought of keeping such a serious secret from Rafiq fueled her guilt.

Fortunately, she would not be forced to choose which course to take in the immediate future. Right now, her focus would be on making Rafiq feel welcome.

She seemed uncomfortable. Rafiq noticed that about Maysa during dinner, and now as they relaxed on rattan sofas in the private courtyard beneath the night sky. Regardless that she seemed on edge, she still looked beautiful as she sat with her legs curled to one side, revealing her bare feet and a delicate silver chain circling one ankle that matched the heavy bangles at her wrists. Her long, dark hair cascaded over her slim shoulders, strands of amber highlighted by the moon, and the sleeveless white gauze dress she wore contrasted with the golden cast of her skin. He remembered touching that skin during a time when they had both been completely captivated by one another. So hungry for each other that it seemed they might never be sated—until the one and only night they crossed the forbidden line and made love.

She captivated him still, fed a fire that he had wrongly assumed would be extinguished by time, mistakes and regrets. He wanted to leave the sofa he had claimed and take the space beside her. He wished to do more than only sit with her. Yet her moratorium on kissing left him with only one option—remain where he sat and simply admire her from afar.

Maysa sighed, her attention focused on the jasmine lining the edge of the stone terrace. "I love summer evenings."

He loved the sound of her voice—soft, lyrical. "You have lost most of your accent."

She smiled, deepening the dimples creasing her cheeks. "The time I spent in the States is responsible for that."

"Do you still know how to speak our native tongue?"

She frowned. "Of course I still know how. I have to communicate with my patients here."

He thought of one question he had wanted to ask. "Why did you return to Bajul to practice medicine knowing how you would be treated following your divorce?"

Her gaze wandered away as she began twisting the bracelets around her right wrist. "Bajul is my home, Rafiq, and since Boutros lives elsewhere, it seemed logical to return. I also missed the quiet pace and the peaceful existence."

"You do not seem at peace tonight," he said. "Is something bothering you?"

She shifted slightly and finally raised her gaze to

his. "Actually, yes. I'm concerned about the lack of care for the poorest in Bajul."

"It is my understanding you are an excellent doctor, therefore they are receiving the finest care."

"But I'm only one person, Rafiq. Other physicians could assist, yet they refuse. They only provide services to those who can pay. It's a travesty."

He understood her frustration, yet he had no solution. "I cannot force other physicians to work for no pay."

"But you could see to it that newer doctors are enticed to come here to fill in the gaps."

He leaned back and set his glass of mango juice on the adjacent table. "How do you propose I do this?"

"By offering government-sponsored grants."

"Our current funds are earmarked for the water conservation efforts. We have no surplus to devote to anything else at this time."

"Then perhaps sell one of the new military planes Adan has recently acquired. It would seem you have more than enough for a country the size of Bajul."

"At times it seems we do not have enough to bolster our defense. But I will take your suggestions into consideration."

He noted a spark of anger in her dark, almond-shaped eyes. "That is all you have to say?"

"Maysa, I am only one voice on the council."

"You are the supreme voice, King Mehdi. You have the last word."

He had less power than she realized. "I must do what the majority dictates to keep the peace."

"At the expense of your people?"

"Again, I will consider your concerns and present

them to the council when it is time to prepare the next budget."

She straightened her legs, planted her feet on the ground, and seared him with a glare. "That is over five months away. People could die before then, both elderly adults and children. Mothers with difficult births."

He did not have the means to accommodate her at this time, yet he could not disappoint her. "I will see what I can do, though I can make no promises."

"I suppose that is enough," she said, her expression somewhat more relaxed. "At least for the time being."

Fatigue began to set in, yet Rafiq could not force himself to leave her. He also could not rid himself of the slight pain resulting from an injury he'd suffered in his youth. He lifted the shoulder slightly, once, twice, before he settled back against the cushions.

"It still bothers you, doesn't it?" Maysa asked.

He was not surprised she had noticed. "What bothers me?"

"Your shoulder. The one you fractured in that ridiculous fight with Aakif Nejem."

"I believe we were fighting over you." He smiled. "And I came away with two black eyes and a lacerated lip. I would have been unscathed had it not been for my falling against the iron gate."

Maysa returned his smile, though she appeared to be attempting to keep it at bay. "The very gate you drove through earlier, designed by my father to ward off unwelcome suitors."

"Yet that gate was not strong enough to keep me from you that night."

A brief span of silence passed between them, as well as an exchanged glance that Rafiq remembered very clearly. The same knowing look they had given each other when he had laid her down in her bed, cloaked only by the cover of darkness, the threat of discovery heightening their desire.

Maysa broke the visual contact first and turned her focus back on the flowers. "That was a long time ago, Rafiq. We were both young and very foolish."

"We were consumed by each other."

She raised a thin brow. "Consumed by lust, you mean."

Had it only been lust, he would have long forgotten that evening. Forgotten her. "Have you never considered what would have happened had your father come upon us?"

"Would he have forced us to marry?" She shook her head. "He would have sent me away from you."

In many ways, that is exactly what had happened. The sultan had sent her into another man's bed. A man who had not deserved her.

When Maysa hid a yawn behind her hand, then stretched her arms above her head, Rafiq suspected she would soon be leaving him again, at least for the evening. "It is time for me to go to bed," she said, confirming his theory. "I have several early visits to make in the village tomorrow."

He struggled for some way to keep her there awhile longer, and returned to the issue that had begun their journey into the past. "Would you examine my shoulder before you retire?"

"What do you believe I'd accomplish by doing that?"

She would be closer to him, at least momentarily. He pressed his palm against the spot that always gave him the most pain. "I would like to see what you think about this ridge. Perhaps you can advise me if it is an issue I need to have evaluated further."

She sighed, rose from the sofa and took the space beside him. "Lean forward." After he complied, she rested her left hand on his left shoulder and examined the offending shoulder with her right hand.

"Well?" he asked.

She pushed against one spot, causing him to wince. "Does that hurt?" she asked.

"Slightly." More than he would allow her to see.

"That's your deltoid muscle," she said as she continued to knead the area. "You have quite a bit of tension there."

The tension behind his fly began to increase with every caress of her fingertips. "Perhaps it is only stress-induced?"

"Perhaps, but I cannot tell for certain without an X-ray. You could probably benefit from physical therapy."

The therapy she was offering him now was quite beneficial in terms of soothing the soreness. He could not say the same for his libido. And when she leaned over and applied more pressure, his palm automatically came to rest on her thigh, immediately above her knee, where he drew small circles with his thumb through the dress's thin material.

Her hand froze midmotion. "What are you doing, Rafiq?"

"Nothing." Not presently.

She released a shuddering breath. "We said no touching."

He inched his palm higher. "You said no kissing."

"Rule two, no touching."

Despite her assertions, he did not bother to lift his hand, and she did not bother to shove it away. "Yet you have been touching me."

"As a physician."

"And I have reacted as any man reacts to a woman's touch."

"For that reason, I should go now."

Rafiq predicted she would stand and leave, but she remained positioned next to him, both hands still resting lightly on his shoulders. He straightened, bringing their faces close, their gazes connecting immediately. He saw the indecision in her eyes, as well as a spark of need.

And then Maysa did something Rafiq did not expect—she broke her first rule.

Three

She had taken complete leave of her senses, but at the moment Maysa didn't care. She only concerned herself with the play of Rafiq's mouth against hers and the impressions he made with the gentle glide of his tongue.

At some point—and she had no idea how or when—he had shifted toward her and she had moved fully into his arms. A nagging voice demanded she stop before she could not, but she disregarded the caution. For once she wanted to be softly kissed, without undue force. Willingly kissed. She wanted to remember how it felt to be a desirable woman, not simply an object of brutal lust.

Yet all the reasons why she shouldn't be doing this kept crowding her mind. She could be only a means to an end for Rafiq. A source of comfort. A temporary diversion. She was also keeping a secret from him. A secret that could ultimately destroy him emotionally, and her reputation literally.

Still, when he cupped her breast, she focused on the sensations, not solid rationale. He traced her nipple with a fingertip, causing her to shift restlessly against the building heat. But when he left her mouth to feather kisses down the column of her throat, sliding the dress's strap down her shoulder, a barrage of bitter memories prompted her to automatically tense.

Rafiq reacted to her sudden change in mood by abruptly rising from the sofa, leaving Maysa alone steeped in self-consciousness. He walked away, his hands laced behind his neck, and stopped in the middle of the terrace, keeping his back to her.

"I'm sorry," Maysa muttered as she readjusted her clothing. "I have no idea what has come over me. We shouldn't be doing this." She'd begun to wonder if she could do it, even if she wanted to.

Rafiq dropped his arms to his sides and faced her again. "I am not sorry, yet I am convinced this will keep happening between us."

So was Maysa, unless she revealed the absolute truth behind her reluctance. She wasn't willing to do that. "We'll simply need to avoid situations such as this. Following dinner each evening, I will return to my quarters, and you will return to yours. We will keep our distance during the day, as well."

He shifted his weight slightly. "And I will lie awake all night, imagining how it would be to touch you with my hands and my mouth in ways I never did when we were younger. I will dream about how it would feel to be buried deep inside you. And each time I see you, I will want the reality."

The heat returned, prompting Maysa to cross her legs. "Then perhaps it would be best if you found another place for your respite."

"I care not to be anywhere else."

Truthfully, she didn't want him to leave, either. "Then I suppose you will be forced to rely solely on your imagination."

"Or we could both choose not to fight our desire. No one would know if we became lovers again."

How very easy it would be to agree. How very foolish if she did. "I would know, Rafiq. Nothing could ever exist between us beyond temporary physical pleasure. You are the king, and I am a woman who most believe is unfit to keep company with you, let alone be your lover."

He rubbed a palm over his nape. "Again, we could be discreet. We could enjoy each other during the time we have."

The fact he didn't say she wasn't unsuitable was as effective as a frigid shower. Maysa stood, hands fisted at her sides, nails digging into her palms. "I have already been one man's whore, Rafiq. I will not be another's."

"I am prisoner to tradition and acceptable mores, Maysa, as are you. Yet that does not mean I would view you as my *sharmuta*."

"Yet that is exactly what I would be to you, a woman not fit to be your queen, yet expected to do your bidding in bed. Answer your every need, yet receive nothing in return, as it was with Boutrous. That would make me your mistress."

Maysa expected to see anger in Rafiq's expression,

but he only seemed concerned. "What did Boutros do to you, Maysa?"

"This has nothing to do with him." Only a partial truth. "This has to do with us. I have developed a great deal of self-respect during our time apart. I am not that smitten schoolgirl who would have given everything to you, knowing I could never have a future with you."

He released a rough sigh. "What do you wish me to say, Maysa?"

That he would tell the elders to go to hell. That she was an acceptable partner by virtue of her intelligence and skills, not her past. That he would make an effort to change the archaic laws governing the role of women. "Nothing, Rafiq. I wish for you to say nothing. You have already said it all."

When she turned to retire to her room, Rafiq called her back. "I would rather die a thousand deaths than to wound you again, Maysa."

And she would experience a thousand more regrets if she gave in to the sincerity in his dark eyes. "Then don't, Rafiq. Be my friend."

He approached her slowly. "I am your friend. That has never changed, despite the distance between us."

Before she made another monumental mistake and walked back into his arms, Maysa left the terrace and returned to her quarters. And once she was safely in bed, she let herself imagine what it would be like to make love with him again, too. Yet the fantasies could never replace the reality. But the reality was she'd invited him here for a reason, and tomorrow she would begin to implement her plan. And with that plan came the opportunity to educate a king. The beautiful, sensual king of her heart.

* * *

Shirtless, Rafiq faced the double-paned window overlooking the veranda, allowing Maysa a premiere view from the partially open door. The strong planes of his broad shoulders, broken by a slight scar on his right, demonstrated he was still as physically fit as he'd always been. The indentation of his spine tracked into the waistband of his navy pajamas, surrounded by supple, golden skin. And below that, narrow hips and a toned buttocks looked quite touchable.

But she wouldn't touch him. Not today. She had more pressing matters at hand, provided he cooperated.

Maysa moved quietly into the room, several items of clothing clutched in her arms. "Did you sleep well?"

If he was at all startled by her appearance, he didn't show it. He simply turned and presented a half smile. "I slept as well as can be expected in a strange bed alone, knowing that a desirable woman is such a short distance away."

She disregarded the innuendo, but she could not seem to keep her eyes off the downward stream of masculine hair below his navel, or that he seemed quite pleased to see her from an anatomical standpoint. "Well," she said as she forced her gaze to his dark eyes, "I hope you are sufficiently rested since I have plans for us today."

"Plans?" He rounded the foot of the bed and stood a few feet from her. "What do these plans entail?"

"I am traveling to the Diya region and I want you to come with me."

He frowned. "That is over two hours away."

"Yes, and I make the journey every Wednesday to

treat the sheep farmers and their families. Today is Wednesday."

"Why would you wish me to accompany you?"

"Because I believe it's important you begin to understand the health care issues facing your country, including the lack of resources in remote areas."

He appeared to mull that over before he spoke again. "The people of Diya never supported my father. It has been reported several possible insurgency camps exist there."

"Perhaps they did not embrace being ignored by your father," she said. "You could change that."

He strolled around the room for a moment before turning to her again. "Would we be able to communicate by cell phone with the outside world?"

She rolled her eyes. "There are no cellular towers. The villagers only recently received regular phone service, and many do not have electricity. Some do not have adequate water supplies."

"If I accompany you, I would require a contingent of guards for both our protection should I be recognized."

"Not if you are unrecognizable." She tossed him the army-green shirt and cargo pants. "If you put these on and wear sunglasses, no one will know a king walks among them."

He unfolded the clothes and inspected them. "I doubt a change of attire would serve as an adequate disguise."

"If you wear sunglasses and shave, that should suffice."

He laughed. A deep, low, sensual laugh that sent chills down the length of Maysa's body. "I have no intention of shaving."

"Your goatee will grow back, Rafiq. Most likely in two days' time."

He leveled his gaze on her. "Is it that important I join you?"

"Yes, and it should be important to you. A good ruler knows his people. Especially the poor and less fortunate."

He sighed. "All right. I will do this for you, but I still believe it is necessary to bring along a guard."

"That isn't necessary. I've traveled the terrain many times and I have yet to encounter any trouble. I also travel with a firearm should I need it."

His grin arrived slowly. "Do you know how to use it?"

She returned his smile. "I'm certain I could shoot straight should the situation arise. So rest assured, as long as you are with me, your royal body will be safe."

"You are willing to take my royal body into your own hands?"

Ignoring the suggestive words, she pointed at the clothes. "Dress, Your Majesty. I'll meet you at the back entrance to the house."

His smile disappeared. "And I will drive."

"No, you will not."

With that, she flipped her hair over one shoulder and left the room to prepare for the journey. With a reluctant king in tow, it could prove to be quite an adventure.

Rafiq had always known Maysa to have an adventurous spirit. He had seen her take risks most women would not dare undertake. Yet he had never seen her dressed as she was now. She wore a long-sleeved white blouse covered by a white laboratory coat, as well as khaki pants and a pair of heavy boots. Her official apparel concealed her feminine attributes, yet her absence of makeup did not take away from her natural beauty. He knew exactly what existed beneath the clothing— full breasts, round bottom, soft skin.

While Rafiq's discomfort began to grow, Maysa looked entirely comfortable behind the wheel of the Hummer, navigating the rugged terrain with practiced ease. He, on the other hand, was sweltering due to the August sun and in part due to his inability to take his eyes off Maysa. Since last evening, he had not been able to escape the memory of her kiss. Could not erase the images of what he wanted to do with her. To her. But he also could not forget her reaction to his touch, as if she had been somewhat repulsed.

He streaked a hand over his forehead and took a drink of water from the canteen she had brought along. "How much farther?"

"We're almost there," she said, keeping her eyes trained on the dirt road. "Over the mountain."

As soon as they topped the rise, Maysa continued down the incline past a tribesman herding sheep and several young boys playing barefoot along the path. Once they arrived in the primitive town, she pulled in front of a large canvas tent where several people had gathered around the opening.

After Maysa shut off the ignition and climbed out, Rafiq remained seated to observe the interaction between doctor and villagers. Women, men and children converged upon her, shouting greetings and presenting smiles that she returned.

After a time, she managed to make her way to the passenger door to address him. "Keep your sunglasses on at all times," she said in a low voice. "I will tell everyone you're from the States and you do not speak Arabic. In fact, it's best if you do not speak at all."

That could take effort. "If that is what you wish."

She favored him with a smile. "And by the way, I like you better clean-shaven."

His hand immediately went to his bare chin. "Be that as it may, I will begin growing it back as soon as we are finished with this adventure. Otherwise, someone might mistake me for my brother."

She pulled a stethoscope from the pocket of the lab coat and draped it around her neck. "Do what you will, Rafiq, but take it from a woman. Kissing a man with a beard is not always comfortable." With that, she rounded the SUV while Rafiq remained to ponder her words. Did she intend to let him kiss her again? One could always hope.

Rafiq slid out of the Hummer and joined Maysa at the rear to haul the large supply trunk into the tent while she carried a smaller medical kit. She signaled him to be seated in a rattan chair in the corner of the tent and pressed a fingertip to her lips, reminding him to be silent, as if he were an errant schoolboy. She then went to work, tending to the villagers with both speed and skill. She periodically handed out treats to the children and advice to worried mothers. Several men stood nearby, eyeing Rafiq with suspicion and occasionally watching Maysa with lust. He could not blame them though he did not care for their leers. Yet defending the physician's honor would most likely incur the physician's wrath.

As Rafiq continued to witness Maysa deliver her expert ministrations, he experienced a sense of pride, though he had no right. He had never discouraged her from entering the medical field, but he had not encouraged her, either. He had always believed she would be destined to abandon her dreams for the life of a sultan's wife. But she had bravely defied convention and custom, and had suffered severe consequences for her choices.

Watching her care for these downtrodden people, receiving their adoration and appreciation, Rafiq realized that perhaps she had not suffered as much as one would believe. Perhaps she was living the life she was meant to live. A life without him.

A commotion coming from the tent's entrance drew his attention. A young man elbowed his way through the awaiting crowd, shouting, *"Tâbeeb!"*

When he rushed toward Maysa, Rafiq immediately shot to his feet to intervene. Maysa gave him a quelling look as she took the farmer aside and spoke to him quietly.

He could not hear most of the conversation, but he understood the gravity of the situation from the concerned look in Maysa's eyes. She turned and addressed the woman who'd been assisting her and instructed her to do what she could until she returned. Then she gestured Rafiq to follow her out of the tent. Once they were back in the SUV, Maysa followed a truck out of the village and toward the mountains.

"Where are we going?" Rafiq asked as Maysa made one hairpin turn without braking.

"There is a woman in labor," she said. "She's having difficulty delivering."

"Her first child?"

"Fourth, and that's what concerns me."

The man had not looked old enough to father four offspring. But he did not have time to voice his opinion as Maysa pulled into a drive leading to an earthen hut. She had stopped the vehicle, retrieved the smallest medical kit and had arrived at the front door before he had barely left the passenger seat.

Rafiq made haste and entered the house to see Maysa disappearing through a door to the right of the living area. He discovered three children sitting on the low blue sofas, their eyes wide with fear. The oldest could not have been more than six years old, the second perhaps four and the youngest about two years of age. He surveyed the room to find it absent of any adult and assumed the father had chosen to be at his wife's side.

When he claimed another smaller sofa to wait, the oldest little girl came to her feet and crossed the room to stand before him.

He remembered Maysa's insistence he not speak, yet he could not pretend he was not concerned over the child's well-being. *"Shu esmek?"*

She twirled a lock of dark hair around her tiny finger. "Aini."

The name suited her, he decided. With her dark curls and equally dark eyes, she was as pretty as a spring flower. He remembered Elena once saying that children only wanted to be fed, clothed and to feel safe. Aini was clothed, she did not appear undernourished, yet he imagined she did not feel secure at the moment.

For that reason, Rafiq began to recite a story about a lost sheep in search of its mother, a tale he had learned from his own mother. One by one, the other children gathered around and listened intently. When they looked at him with complete trust, he realized, though he had been born to royalty, he had never felt quite as important as he did now. He also experienced a fierce need to protect them. The protection he had not afforded his unborn child.

The sound of mournful moans began to filter from the adjacent room, thrusting away the regret. Rafiq waved the children onto the sofa beside him and set the youngest in his lap. He raised his voice in an attempt to muffle the scream that made his blood run cold. He could only imagine what these innocents were feeling at the moment—hearing their mother in such abject pain.

Maysa emerged from the chamber holding a bundle in her arms, a cap of dark hair showing from beneath the white blanket. To Rafiq, she looked completely natural holding a baby, and in one fleeting moment, he imagined her holding his child.

She approached the sofa and smiled. "Here is your baby brother," she said to the children in Arabic, followed by, "The baby was breech," in English, directed at Rafiq. "The mother has lost a lot of blood and needs a hospital."

While the two oldest children slid off the sofa to view their new sibling, Rafiq moved the youngest child from his lap and stood. "Is the mother in danger?"

"Yes."

Her somber tone demonstrated to Rafiq the gravity of the situation. "How much time does she have?"

"I fear not long enough to make the three-hour drive, but we have no choice."

Rafiq would give her another choice. "Is there a telephone?"

Maysa looked around the room and pointed at an

ancient handset hanging from the wall. "There, though I cannot guarantee it works."

He would soon find out. Fortunately, the telephone was operable, though it took several attempts to connect with the palace, and another two to convince the staff he was in fact the king. Finally, he managed to reach his brother. "Adan, I need your immediate assistance."

"You have bedded Maysa and you need to know how to proceed?"

He was in no mood to put up with Adan's questionable comments. "I need a medevac helicopter sent to Diya immediately. Make certain to have medics onboard, and that it arrives in less than fifteen minutes."

"What is this about, Rafiq?"

"A woman's life is at stake," he said. "We have only a small window of time to deliver her to the hospital."

"I will do the best that I can on such short notice."

"You will do exactly what I say, and you will be expedient!"

"Calm down, Rafiq. I will have the helicopter there in ten minutes, even if I must fly it myself."

"Good. I am counting on you, Adan."

As soon as he hung up, Rafiq recognized his heart had been racing at breakneck speed. He had done what he could and hoped that it would be enough. He had not been able to save his own wife, but perhaps he could save this one.

Even after she'd treated the last remaining patient in the tent, Maysa could not recall feeling so utterly helpless. A few hours ago, she'd watched the helicopter fly away while she stayed behind since there hadn't been room for her and the woman's husband. "I should have left for the hospital hours ago."

Rafiq came up behind her and rested his palms on her shoulders. "She is in competent hands," he said. "The hospital was prepared to receive them immediately. I am certain all will be well."

If only she could feel so confident. "I hope so," she said as she gathered supplies and put them in the kit. "I cannot imagine how her poor husband would feel if he lost his wife, not to mention having to raise four children on his own."

"It is not something you would wish to imagine," he said. "So do not."

Maysa understood all too well what Rafiq was probably feeling at that moment—his own loss. "I hope we receive some news soon."

"Adan said he would find a way to get word to us when there was news to report."

Maysa was grateful Rafiq had been there to offer support, and thankful that his position had opened doors she would not have been able to open herself. She turned with a smile and handed him the kit. "Please put this in the Hummer and we'll be on our way."

"We cannot leave now."

He couldn't be serious. She was so tired she could barely stand. "Why would we wish to stay any longer? I've finished with my work here for the week."

He smiled. "I have been told the villagers have arranged a feast in honor of the *Tâbeeb* and her *American* friend."

As much as Maysa would like to attend, she was simply too tired for a celebration. "As it stands now, we won't be home until midnight."

"You have not eaten all day."

"I had some goat cheese and *lahvash*."

He frowned. "Would you insult those who have prepared a fine meal in your honor?"

Before Maysa could respond, "I wouldn't if I were you, Dr. Barad" came from behind her.

She glanced back to see a tall, lanky, sandy-haired man with a full beard approaching. A familiar face she hadn't seen in quite some time.

As soon as he came to her side, Maysa drew him into an embrace. "It is so good to see you, Jerome."

He set her back and surveyed her face. "It's good to see you, too, Maysa. It's been at least a month."

"Longer," she said with a smile. "I assumed you returned to Canada."

"I did for a time, but I didn't stay long. After making a few stops, I'm back in Diya to finish my work."

After Maysa heard Rafiq clear his throat, she faced him again. "Jerome Forte, this is…" She struggled to come up with a proper—and false—introduction. "This is Rafe."

Jerome presented a cynical smile. "No. This is Rafiq Mehdi, ruling king of Bajul."

She should have known she wouldn't be able to put anything over on the photographer. "You're right, but I prefer you keep his identity to yourself."

"You may count on my absolute discretion," he said before he regarded Rafiq once more. "It is a pleasure to meet you, Your Majesty."

Rafiq stared at Jerome's extended hand for a few moments before accepting the gesture. "What brings you to this part of the world, Mr. Forte?"

"Please, it's Jerome." He wrapped an arm around

Maysa's waist, much to her chagrin. "I've been photographing the area for an international magazine. Not only did Maysa suggest the region, she has been instrumental in convincing the villagers here to allow me to take their pictures."

Rafiq looked as though he might throw a punch. "Is that all she's been assisting you with?"

She moved away from Jerome and frowned. "Yes, that is all. Jerome and I have been friends for several years."

"Yes, we have," Jerome said as he smiled down on her. "And I've missed our talks."

"We must decide whether we are staying or going," Rafiq said, a definite edge in his tone. "If you choose to leave, then we must do so now."

He suddenly sounded as if he wanted to leave. "We should stay for a while," she said. "You're right. I wouldn't want to seem ungrateful."

Rafiq moved beside her and possessively took her arm. "If you will excuse us, Mr. Forte, we have a celebration to attend."

"As do I," Jerome said. "The party is being held a block away. We can all walk together."

Considering the disapproving look on Rafiq's face, Maysa was somewhat concerned that accompanying Jerome could lead to trouble. She would certainly hate to have to intervene, though she would. She did not appreciate male posturing in any form or fashion. "Then I suppose we should be going before the sun has completely set."

The trio walked the brick streets of the village, Maysa flanked by the men. While Rafiq remained stoic and silent, Jerome chatted nonstop about his recent travels to Tunisia. Fortunately they arrived at the expansive field without incident.

Several fires blazed throughout the area, providing the means to cook the fare for the feast, including spits with roasting lamb. She'd never cared for that delicacy due to her fondness for baby sheep. But tonight she would sample everything to avoid appearing unappreciative.

As they wove their way through the throngs of people, Maysa answered each greeting with one of her own as Rafiq and Jerome hung back. The village men wore summer-weight *bishts,* their heads covered by *mashadahs,* while the women wore the usual *hijab.* She, Rafiq and Jerome seemed out of place in their civilian clothes, yet no one seemed to notice—except for a group of young women who stood to the side of the banquet table, giggling behind their hands when the men walked up to fill their plates.

Maysa leaned toward Rafiq and whispered, "You are making quite an impression on the female population here. Perhaps you could find a suitable wife among them."

"Perhaps you have discovered a suitable lover in your Canadian friend."

She found the jealousy in his voice somewhat amusing. "As I have told you, Jerome is only a friend. Nothing more."

He kept filling a bowl full of *ogdat* until the stew almost overflowed from the vessel. "He would like more. He would like to have you all to himself."

"Don't be foolish, Rafiq. If you'll look to your left you'll notice he is preoccupied with a young woman as we speak."

Rafiq followed Maysa's gaze to where Jerome was standing near one of the fire pits, charming a pretty young woman who seemed to be hanging on his every word, as well as his arm. "She does not appear to be more than a teenager," he said.

"I predict she is well over the age of consent," she said. "And interested in Jerome. I've seen them together before."

Rafiq frowned. "Her parents approve of this liaison with a foreigner?"

She sighed. "I have no idea, and it is not any of my concern. Now let's eat so we can leave as soon as possible."

Maysa followed Rafiq to the nearest fire and sat beside him on the ground. They ate their meal in silence, then afterward watched several men perform the *dabke* in their honor. As badly as she wanted to leave, she felt it would be impolite to depart during the dance. A dance that seemed to go on and on for an eternity.

By the time the group had finished, and the applause had died down, Maysa worried she could fall asleep and land face-forward in the fire. "We should go now, otherwise I might be forced to let you drive."

Rafiq regarded his watch. "It is late. Perhaps we should find lodging here for the night."

Finding herself in a hotel room with Rafiq did not seem wise. "As far as I know, Diya has no inns."

"Is there a family who would take us in?"

"The two of you can use my tent, Your Excellency."

Once more, Jerome had interrupted the discourse by stealing into the area without Maysa's notice. "Then where would you sleep, Jerome?" she asked, though she knew the answer.

He grinned. "I have made other accommodations."

Of course he had—with the young woman who happened to be standing behind him. "I appreciate the offer, but from what I recall, your tent is not that large." At least not large enough to house two former lovers battling chemistry.

"I disagree," he said. "It's very large, and it has enough room for three people, provided you're willing to sleep side by side on the ground. Actually, there's a sleeping bag covering the ground, and a spare should you need it. It's really quite comfortable."

"I really don't think—"

"I believe it will be suitable for the evening," Rafiq chimed in. "We appreciate your generosity, and we accept."

Maysa momentarily gaped. "I don't accept. I am quite capable of driving."

"You are exhausted," Rafiq said. "As am I. We will rise early in the morning and return refreshed and fully awake."

She doubted she would sleep at all with Rafiq in such close proximity. "I truly don't believe it's necessary."

"His Majesty has a point, Maysa," Jerome added. "There's no need to hurry home when you have a perfectly good tent for the night. It's in the same location, so I'm sure you'll have no problem finding it."

With that, Jerome took his paramour's hand and disappeared into the darkness.

Maysa brought her attention back to Rafiq. "I'm not certain it's wise for us to spend the night together in a tent."

"And I do not think it is wise to drive hours in a state of exhaustion."

She decided to give up on that argument, in part because she was extremely tired. "All right, you may have the shelter and I will sleep in the Hummer."

"No one is sleeping in the Hummer, Maysa. We are both adults and I vow to maintain control, if that is your concern."

That was precisely her concern. "Do you promise to stay on your side of the tent?"

He raised a hand as if taking an oath. "I promise that I will be the gentleman Elena has taught me to be."

Could she trust that he was telling the truth? Could she trust herself around him? Of course she could. She would keep her distance, and demand he keep his. And in the morning, she would return home without any regrets.

"All right. We'll stay in the tent."

And she sincerely hoped it *was* big enough for both of them.

Four

The shelter was much larger than Rafiq had envisioned, and not a tent in the true sense of the word. The structure was comprised of a wooden frame covered by canvas, and tall enough to allow him to stand. Yet it seemed much too small for a man who greatly desired the woman with whom he would share the space.

As he sat on the blanket-covered ground to remove his boots, Maysa stood in the corner, washing her face in a basin set out on a small side table. She had removed her blouse, leaving her clad in a fitted, sleeveless undershirt. While he continued to watch her, she slipped the band securing the braid, unwound it and then shook out her hair that cascaded down her back, the ends touching the top of her waist. He recalled that fall of hair surrounding him, flowing over his bare skin. How many nights had he imagined it happening again? Too numerous to count. And when he had made love to Rima, Maysa had oftentimes been foremost in his mind, fueling his fantasies. A shameful secret he would carry to the grave.

Maysa turned and stretched her hands above her head, drawing the shirt tighter, revealing she wore no bra. She removed a brush from her bag and ran it through her hair. "Thank you for all you did today. And be sure to thank Adan for getting word to us that both mother and child received a clean bill of health."

"Do not forget your part in that good news," he said as he followed the movement of her hand sliding the brush through her long locks, back and forth.

"I was only doing my job."

She was clearly bent on torturing him at the moment.

He stripped away his own shirt for the sake of comfort, and as soon as she turned off the lantern, he intended to remove his pants, also for comfort. If that somehow offended her, then so be it. After all, she had made certain their makeshift beds were almost a meter apart. Still, the distance would not prevent his fantasies, or discourage him if she gave him the least bit of encouragement.

Wise or not, he wanted her still. He would continue to want her even after they parted ways. Yet her reaction the night before when he touched her indicated she did not want him as fiercely as he wanted her, if at all.

After replacing the brush in the duffel, Maysa returned to the pallets, lowered herself onto the blankets and crossed her legs before her. "Are you tired?"

Sleep was the last thing on his mind with Maysa so close. "Surprisingly I am not."

"Neither am I. I thought perhaps we could talk."

He stretched out on his side facing her, and bent his elbow to support his jaw with his hand. "What do you wish to talk about?"

"Your relationship with Rima."

He had not expected that, nor did he care to discuss it. "She was my wife for a brief time and that is all that needs to be said."

"Actually, that's what I wanted to talk about. Why did you wait so long to marry her?"

He had had many reasons, but he chose to omit one—he had hoped Rima would eventually tire of waiting. "I attended university, and when I returned, I had to assist my father since Zain had left for the States. We had no indication when he would return, or even if he would return at that point."

"That seems like a logical justification for a man, but I don't understand why Rima would agree to delay a wedding for the sake of duty when your responsibility would still exist after the wedding."

Rima had never pressured him to set a date. He had done so only because it had been expected. "She decided to travel and then after her father passed, she spent a good deal of time with her mother. We were both in no hurry." And they had both believed they had a lifetime to spend together. A life that would include polite conversation and little passion.

"I would say that's obvious," Maysa said. "You waited almost fifteen years to make it official."

In many ways, fifteen years had not been long enough. "I understand why you would be confused over the decision, considering you married Boutros almost immediately after the betrothal."

Her gaze faltered. "I wasn't given a choice. My father demanded I marry him immediately, per the terms of the agreement. Boutros wasn't getting any younger, and he wanted an heir."

"An heir you did not give him."

"Fortunately, no."

When Maysa began to rub her right wrist, only then did Rafiq notice the ropelike scar circling it. When he had called on her the first night, she had been wearing heavy bangles that concealed the mark. Tonight, the wound was uncovered and he needed to know its origination, though he suspected he already did.

He immediately sat upright and took her hand to study it further. "What is this?"

She wrenched out of his grasp. "It's nothing."

He needed more evidence to substantiate his theory. "Take off your watch."

"No."

"Then I shall do it for you."

He anticipated she would fight him when he unbuckled the strap, yet she sat motionless with a blank stare, as if shielding herself from the truth he sought. And he found that truth when he removed the watch— another circular scar.

Rafiq bit back his anger and tempered his tone. "Did he bind you, Maysa?"

"Rafiq, I—"

"Did that *kalet* tie you?"

"Yes!" she said, her voice heralding her fury. "Yes, the bastard bound me. He grew tired of me fighting him."

Rafiq gritted his teeth and spoke through them. "He forced himself on you against your will?"

"Yes, he did, and he also did this." She twisted around and raised the back of her shirt, revealing a series of slashes across her flesh. "He tried to beat me into submission, and when it did not work, he would go for the rope."

Unable to remain still, Rafiq stood and began pacing the area. He longed for a solid wall to hit, a means to expend his rage. "I will kill him with my own hands."

Maysa's laughter spun him around. "You are too late to ride to my rescue, I fear. It's my understanding his heart is failing, though I'm surprised to learn he has a heart at all. I have no doubt it is as black as midnight."

Rafiq returned to her and claimed the space beside her. "Did you not mention this to your father?"

"Yes, I did. He told me that to be a good wife, I would do what was required. Even Shamil sided with him."

His respect for the sultan and his former friend plummeted. "And your mother?"

"She always left the room, most likely to hide her tears. But I never cried. I was determined not to let any of them see my tears or my weakness, especially Boutros."

"Yet you suffered for your strength."

She raised her chin, defiance reflecting from her eyes. "I called on that well-honed strength the night I left him."

He needed to know all the details, both bad and good. "How did you manage to escape?"

"We were at his home in Oman. He was out with one of his many mistresses. I broke into his desk, stole several thousand riyals and caught a plane to Canada. That's where I first met Jerome, on the plane. He assisted me in finding temporary housing. He was also instrumental in finding me employment. I worked as a waitress in a busy café, and once I'd saved enough money, I traveled to the States and began my studies."

Her resilience amazed him. "Your father never offered financial assistance?"

"Of course not. He was furious. But my mother eventually sent me money whenever she could. She enabled me to hire an attorney for the divorce. And as they say, the rest is history."

He formed his palm to her face. "Though I admire what you have accomplished on your own, you should have come to me for help."

"Why would I do that, Rafiq? You all but bid me a final farewell after we spent that one night together, or have you forgotten?"

The bitterness in her tone caused him to drop his hand. "I have never forgotten that night." Nor had he forgotten the sorrow in her eyes when he had told her they could not be together again.

"You told me we would remain friends," she said. "Yet we never really spoke again."

"We were forbidden to have any contact."

"We were forbidden after you were officially betrothed to Rima, but that didn't stop you from taking my virginity, did it?"

"And I recall you came to me willingly that night. You begged me to make love to you."

She lowered her eyes. "Yes, I did, and I never regretted it. I only regretted…"

He raised her chin with his fingertips, forcing her to look at him. "You regretted what?"

"That we only had that one time. But it was enough

to get me through those horrendous times with Boutros. I would close my eyes and escape back to that night. I reminded myself that what we shared was pure and good, not ugly and brutal. Those memories helped ease the pain and tolerate the reminders I still carry with me."

He suspected her internal scars still ran deep. "I did the same with Rima," he said, surprised at how easily the admission flowed out of his mouth. "She came to me willingly, and I always treated her with care and respect. Yet I sensed her thoughts were somewhere else. Perhaps on someone else, as were mine. I always thought of you."

"And the women before Rima?"

"I always imagined you. And the men after Boutros?"

"There have been no other men."

Perhaps that should not surprise him. "No one?"

"No. When you kissed me the other night, that was the first time since I left him. I thought I was immune to desire, but you proved me wrong." She attempted a smile but it faded quickly. "Although when you touched me, I realized I still have lingering issues."

He had mistakenly believed she had no intention of returning his affection. "I understand why you would feel that way, but I would have hoped the passage of time would have aided in your healing."

Her hand went to her wrist again, as if she needed to remember. "My emergency room rotations served as a constant reminder of what I had endured. I treated women who had suffered the same, and I began to realize that marital violence spans all cultures. Some still turn a blind eye to the problem because they believe that a wife should persevere to save the marriage. Fortunately, I was wise enough to leave."

He took her hand again and kissed her palm. "You were brave, Maysa. You still are. Braver than most men."

He saw the first sign of tears in her eyes, but she quickly blinked them away. "I am also damaged, Rafiq. No man would want me."

I want you. "You are a beautiful, desirable woman, *habibti.* Any man would be fortunate to have you."

"Well, I do not intend to give anyone that option. But I do have a favor to ask of you."

"Whatever you wish."

"Would you hold me tonight?"

She asked so little of him, yet so much. "If that is what you desire."

"But can you only hold me without wanting more?"

He could offer her a lie, or be completely honest, which is what she deserved. "If I said I did not wish to make love with you again, that would be untrue. But I will honor your request and be satisfied having you in my arms as we sleep. Shall I turn off the lantern?"

"I'd prefer to leave it on."

To chase away the demons, Rafiq presumed. "Then we will leave it on."

She stretched out on her back and sent him a sincere smile. "Then, Your Majesty, you are cordially invited to join me for an evening of celibacy."

He returned her smile, despite his disappointment. "I accept your invitation, Dr. Barad, as long as you do not steal the blankets."

"I will try to refrain."

When Maysa shifted to her side, Rafiq covered them

both and slid his arm beneath her. He decided to remain clothed from the waist down, at least until he was assured she slept. Then he would strip off his slacks and hope she did not notice.

Yes, she was inadvertently bent on torturing him with her request. And with the floral scent of her hair teasing his senses, her warm body fitted to his, she had succeeded in her mission.

At some point during the night, Maysa roused from a fitful sleep to the sound of steady breathing. A few moments passed before she became fully awake and turned to find Rafiq lying on his back. The lantern had begun to dim, washing his bare chest in an amber glow, yet allowing her to covertly study him. Human anatomy had been a part of her daily existence for years, but she was not immune to prime physical specimens, and the king definitely fit into that category.

His right arm curled above his head on the pillow and the other rested at his side between them. His dark lashes fanned out beneath his closed eyes, and his lips were pressed together. His clean-shaven jaw had already begun to show the signs of a light spattering of whiskers.

She continued her visual journey down the column of his throat and on to the prominent pectorals that indicated he still worked out with weights. He'd developed that passion in his teen years, while his brothers had stayed in shape picking up women, literally and figuratively, according to Rafiq. He had been a serious student, so bent on earning his father's respect. Bent on being his father in many ways. Yet she had known a different prince, the one who had spoken sweet words in soft whispers. The young man who had touched and kissed her so gently.

Those memories prompted her to reach out and touch him now. She sifted through the triangular shading on his sternum and slid a fingertip lightly down his belly, pausing where the sheet was draped loose and low, covering his hips. Realization that she didn't see a waistband dawned on her. She rose up to view his pants piled in a heap at the end of the pallet. Only his pants?

Morbid female curiosity caused her to lift the sheet to take a peek.

Hello…

As she suspected, he was unequivocally—and beautifully—bare. And for some reason, she could not quit staring.

"Are you enjoying the sight?"

She dropped the sheet and glanced up to see Rafiq's half smile and his open eyes full of amusement. "You're naked."

He propped a bent arm behind his neck. "I am, and you seem quite fascinated by that fact."

His voice hinted at arrogance and pride and Maysa had to admit, he had much to be proud of. "The question is, why did you take off your pants?"

"I always remove them when I am in bed. Otherwise, I have difficulty sleeping. You do not remember this?"

Oh, yes, she did, though they had only slept together one time. "I remember."

"Do you wish me to put them back on?"

Did she? "I wouldn't want you to be uncomfortable on my account, Your Excellency."

"Good. Feel free to carry on, although should you

proceed, you are in danger of waking the sleeping dragon."

She sent a downward glance to the place she'd recently inspected. "I believe the dragon has already been roused."

His grin expanded. "And you are surprised by this?"

Not in the least, but she was surprised by her reaction. She felt winded and flushed and…needy. "I apologize for touching you without your permission."

"Never apologize for something so pleasurable. I am yours to do with what you will."

She so badly wanted to return to the time when she had been secure in her sensuality. When she hadn't been afraid to explore, or be explored. She had the perfect guide next to her, a man she could trust. A man she had desired for as long as she could recall. Perhaps he couldn't promise a future, but he could bring her back to that land known as the living. First, she had to ask.

"I have a request for you," she said.

"Your wish is my command."

Before she reconsidered, Maysa sat up, drew in a deep breath, pulled her undershirt over her head and tossed it aside. "I want you to touch me the way you did when we were young, Rafiq."

Obvious desire, as well as a cast of concern, called out from his coal-colored eyes. "Are you certain?"

She stretched out on her back, closed her eyes and fisted her hands at her sides. "As long as we go slowly. I need—"

"I understand what you need," he said. "And you may rest assured I will treat you with the greatest of care. You only need tell me to stop, and I will."

She knew he would, otherwise she would never allow this to happen.

After Maysa nodded, Rafiq took her arm, unclenched her hand, and kissed her palm. He then leaned over and kissed her forehead, then each cheek before brushing his lips over hers. "Open your eyes for me." When she complied, he added, "I want you to see me touching you. I want you to know it is me."

He did understand, she realized, and she loved him for it.

Loved him...

She would take that out and examine it later. At the moment, her attention was drawn to Rafiq as he brushed his knuckles down her throat. He circled a fingertip around one breast, then the other, all the while keeping his gaze trained on hers. He seemed to be gauging her reaction, and she reacted with an increase in her respiration. He placed a kiss between her breasts, then sought her eyes again before he dipped his head and closed his mouth over her nipple. The circular movement of his tongue, the gentle pull, caused her to shift restlessly from the sensations. She was so lost in the heat, the yearning, she hadn't realized he was caressing her abdomen. She wanted him to keep going, yet when he slipped the button on her fly, illogical fear enveloped her.

"Stop." Her command came out in a raspy whisper.

But she'd been forceful enough to cause Rafiq to raise his head, taking the welcome warmth of his mouth away from her breast. "Do you wish me to stop completely?"

"Yes... No..." She streaked both hands over her

face. "I'm not certain. A part of me is still fearful, and I despise feeling this way."

"I do not want you to be afraid. I want you to feel only pleasure."

She lowered her eyes. "I know. I'm sorry."

"Do not apologize, Maysa. I promised I would stop when you asked, and I am a man of my word."

She finally looked at him. "You're a good man, Rafiq, and always patient with me."

"I will continue to be patient," he said. "You will determine if you wish to continue. Now we should sleep. We have a long drive ahead of us in the morning."

She didn't want to think about morning. She wasn't certain she could sleep. "I suppose you're right."

"First, may I kiss you?"

How odd that he'd asked, yet she appreciated that he had. "Yes, you may."

"You are not concerned with the no-kissing rule?"

She couldn't help but smile. "I believe it's too late to enforce that now."

"I want to make certain you have not changed your mind."

"I will if you do not hurry up and kiss me."

He rolled her toward him, framed her face with his palms and pressed his lips against hers softly. Yet it didn't last long before Rafiq pulled back and smiled. "Now if you would please put your shirt back on, I might possibly be able to sleep."

Feeling strangely wicked, Maysa leaned over him to retrieve her top, intentionally rubbing her bare breasts against his chest. She rose up and replaced the shirt slower than necessary. "Is that better?"

He swallowed hard. "Somewhat. Should I put on my pants?"

"I'm a doctor, Rafiq. I've seen quite a few naked men in the course of my medical career." In afterthought she added, "But I would prefer you keep the dragon covered."

Rafiq laughed then. A grainy, sensual laugh that almost had her reconsidering sleep. But she wasn't ready to move forward in their intimacy. At least not yet.

When she settled back onto the blanket, Rafiq again folded her in his arms, providing the security she needed at the moment.

Concerned over the future, Maysa listened to the cadence of Rafiq's breathing and determined he wasn't sleeping. "Are you awake?"

"Yes."

"After all the years, I still feel a connection between us. Do you?"

"Of course," he said. "Time does have a way of standing still when it involves friendship."

Friendship... That said it all. "Where do we go from here?"

He brushed a kiss across her forehead. "Wherever we choose to go. And wherever that might be, I promise we will both find pleasure in the journey."

Did she dare continue with this dangerous emotional game? Did she risk losing herself to him again? Yes. She was no longer that starstruck young girl with unattainable dreams. She could never play a role in his future, but she could be a part of his present. They needed each other. He needed comfort, and she needed confidence.

Wise or not, she would make love with him again, provided she wasn't too broken.

Five

He was surprised she had allowed him to drive. He was more surprised by her current demeanor.

As Rafiq navigated the barren terrain, he afforded Maysa an occasional glance. At the moment, her face was turned toward the morning sky shining in through the moon roof, her unbound hair blowing back in the breeze from the open window. He could not see her eyes, now covered with sunglasses, but he could definitely see her smile and the twin dimples framing her mouth. She had also left her blouse unbuttoned, providing a view of the undershirt drawn tight over her breasts. That had almost proved enough distraction to cause him to veer onto the shoulder, coming dangerously close to the edge of the cliff.

Freedom...

That word immediately came to Rafiq's mind. Both yearned for it, yet Maysa captured the essence of it. He wished to see more of that absence of inhibition in the near future. He wanted more of what they had shared last night. Most important, he wanted revenge on the man who had stolen her security and left her scarred for life. Death was not good enough for Boutros Kassab.

"We should keep driving past the city," Maysa said, turning her vibrant smile on him. "We should escape and not tell anyone where we're going."

Her enthusiasm was contagious, and familiar. Many times in their shared pasts they had spoken about this very thing. "And where do you suggest we go?"

She lifted her shoulders in a shrug. "I don't know. South to the sea, maybe. Or perhaps we could travel north into Saudi. Dine at the finest restaurants and stay at the best resort."

He only wished they could be that carefree. "You have responsibilities, as do I."

She frowned. "What happened to your sense of adventure?"

"Replaced by the crown." Determined by duty.

"That, Rafiq, is a travesty." She pointed to his left. "Pull over up there."

She'd indicated a thirty-meter expanse of dirt breaking into the pavement and a sheer drop-off beyond. "Why?"

"Please, just do it. And back into the spot."

Far be it for him to question Maysa once she had her mind set on something. He slowed the Hummer, pulled off to the side of the road and then put the vehicle in Reverse. He made certain to leave sufficient room between the SUV and the drop-off, though he was tempted to inch close enough to earn a scolding.

Once they had stopped, Rafiq shut off the ignition

and draped one hand over the wheel. "Do you wish to watch the traffic the go by?"

She unbuckled her seat belt and opened the door. "No. We're going to sit for a while and look at the mountains."

When Maysa exited, Rafiq did the same and followed her to the back of the vehicle. She opened the tailgate, boosted herself up onto it, and patted the space beside her.

They sat quietly for a time, staring off into the distance. He had seen the panorama countless times, yet he had often taken the majestic mountains for granted. They served as a fortress surrounding the city, nature's protection against those who envied Bajul's peaceful existence and autonomy, as well as its resources.

"You can see the palace from here," Maysa said, breaking into silence. "And of course, who could miss *Mabruk*. We should take a day to explore there before your respite is over."

He did not care to consider the ending of his time with her, though it was inevitable. "When Zain and Madison visited the mountain, they returned with not one but two souvenirs. Zain knew the possible consequences, and he chose to take that risk regardless."

"You don't truly believe that fertility mythology, do you?" she asked.

Perhaps not, but he did not wish to take any undue chances. "I only know the villagers still believe it."

"Well, I can't say that I do. It takes more than a mountain to make a baby."

He sent her a teasing smile. "I was not aware of that."

She playfully swiped at his arm. "I'm certain you don't need me to explain the procreation process."

He rubbed his chin and pretended to think. "I would not object to hearing it in terms I would understand."

She laid a hand above her breast. "Why, Your Majesty, are you asking me to talk dirty to you?"

Precisely. "It would not be the first time if you did."

A blush colored her cheeks. "I was incredibly young back then."

"And extremely bold." He still recalled that night when she had verbalized what she had wanted him to do to her, causing him to shift against the uncomfortable effects of that memory. "I appreciated your candor, and I would hope you still feel that you may say anything to me."

"I do, and I have." She leaned back and supported herself on straight arms. "Do you remember that night when we spent several hours not far from here, looking at the same view?"

He remembered it well. "The night you stole your father's car and whisked me away from the palace?"

"I borrowed his car," she corrected.

"Without his knowledge or permission."

She looked extremely proud of her subterfuge. "I returned it later, and he was never the wiser."

"True. Do you remember the code we used when you would summon me?"

Her smile gave the rising sun competition. "How's the weather. And you would always answer—"

"Hot." And that would start the scramble to find a way to be together.

The silence returned, this time rife with tension as

they centered their gazes on each other. She finally favored him with a smile. "How is the weather?"

"Hotter than a desert blaze."

She leaned to his ear and whispered, "So am I."

He answered the obvious invitation with a kiss. Maysa responded with the passion Rafiq had learned to appreciate years before, and had greatly missed. He had never received the same reaction from his wife, but then their kisses had been obligatory. Absent of passion or undeniable need.

He experienced all those emotions with Maysa, and the intense desire to have her again overwhelmed him. He slid his hand beneath the back of her blouse to feel her bare skin against his palms. She surprised him by guiding that hand around to her breast. The desperate sound she made when he feathered his thumb across her nipple was almost his undoing.

Momentarily releasing her, he shoved the medical kits aside to make a place for them. No words were spoken as they crawled inside the vehicle and immediately moved back into each other's arms. He kissed her again, harder, deeper, as he divided her legs with his knee until they were completely twined together as tightly as braided rope.

"I want to touch you," he said. "Everywhere."

"I want you to touch me." Her voice was winded, her eyes hazy. "I need you to touch me."

The reality sudden dawned. How easy it would be to grant her wish. And unwise. Should anyone come upon them on the verge of making love, the scandal would rock the country. A scandal neither could afford.

He placed a kiss on her forehead. "Not here. Not now. You deserve better than this." That all-important next step would be best taken in a feather bed, not in the bed of an SUV. "We are less than twenty minutes away from your home."

"I'm not sure I can wait another twenty minutes."

Neither was Rafiq. "Then perhaps we should leave immediately."

"Are you sure you wouldn't rather stay here?"

He kissed her again, this time with more restraint to prevent rousing the dragon again. "I am sure. We will have the entire evening to spend together and a bed at our disposal. Provided you are ready to take that next step."

Her smile expanded, showing her dimples to full advantage. "Then what are we waiting for?"

Fortunately, they had waited long enough not to have their burgeoning affair confirmed by another member of the royal family. Had they arrived ten minutes earlier, Zain and Madison Mehdi might have caught them in a thoroughly compromising position.

Maysa wasn't altogether unhappy to see the couple, though their timing wasn't exactly the best. But when they'd come upon Zain and Madison in the living area, both looking extremely serious, she worried this might not be only a casual visit.

Rafiq crossed the room and targeted his brother with a glare. "Why are you here?"

Zain rose from the sofa, his gaze honed in on Maysa. "We have simply stopped by to see how the two of you are getting along."

"That's not true," Madison said as she stood. "We're here because all hell is breaking loose back at the palace."

Maysa exchanged a wary look with Rafiq before she brought her attention back to Madison. "What exactly do you mean?"

"Although arranging for the helicopter was noble, Rafiq," Zain began, "you might have been a bit more discreet. It seems the media has learned you were in Diya with Maysa. You might have made us privy to your plans so that we would have been prepared for the fallout."

"Rafiq had nothing to do with it," Maysa said. "This was all my idea. Had I known it would create a scandal, I would never have considered it."

With his eyes flashing anger, and his hands fisted at his sides, Rafiq looked as if he might fly into a rage. "I was in Diya observing one of Bajul's finest doctors treating the sick and downtrodden. What scandal is there in that?"

Madison lowered herself onto the sofa and folded her hands together. "Because rumor has it you spent the night with the country's finest doctor."

Searing heat began to work its way from Maysa's throat to her forehead. "We slept together in a tent." Could that have sounded more questionable? "In a large tent, and all we did was sleep." Excluding some minor foreplay and major kissing. Hopefully they wouldn't ask about the ride back from Diya.

"Did anyone see you together on your return from Diya?" Zain asked.

Clearly that had been too much for Maysa to hope for. "No one saw us."

"There was nothing to see," Rafiq interjected, sounding a bit too defensive in Maysa's opinion.

"Everyone, please sit," Madison said. "We need to implement a plan."

Rafiq slid his hands into his pants' pockets and remained frozen on the spot. "I prefer to stand."

Maysa preferred to leave for the closest exit, but she claimed the chair adjacent to the sofa before she answered that urge. "What do you suggest we do about this misunderstanding?"

Zain draped an arm over his wife's shoulder. "Madison held a press conference this morning to—"

"Without my permission?" Rafiq interjected.

Maysa affected the calm Rafiq failed to show. "What did this press conference entail?"

"Attempting to answer the usual questions," Madison said. "What business did the king have in Diya? What is the true relationship between the king and doctor? In other words, are they having a sordid affair? Nothing I haven't faced before in my career."

"I really feel badly you're having to work on your holiday, Madison," Maysa said.

Zain kissed Madison's cheek. "Even after blessing me with two babies, my wife is still the best at what she does."

Madison smiled. "Sweetheart, I can lactate and change a thousand diapers a day and still handle my job. That's part of why you love me."

This time Zain kissed her on the mouth. "And you love me for my overt charm, as well as my royal staff."

While Maysa couldn't hold back her laughter, Rafiq grumbled an Arabic curse. "Could the two of you stop mooning over each other and bring your minds back to the issues at hand?" he said. "Specifically, I demand to know every detail of this press conference."

Maysa could only guess at that, but she was certain karma had arrived, telling her to steer clear of any intimacy with the king. Steer clear of him altogether. "I would assume Madison denied the conjecture, Rafiq."

Madison shrugged. "Of course. I said the king wanted to investigate medical care in the outlying villages, and that's why he accompanied Dr. Barad to Diya. He preferred to do so anonymously to allow him a better advantage. I ignored any questions about the sleeping arrangements."

"Madison successfully dodged those bullets," Zain added. "But there will be plenty more if someone discovers the two of you cohabiting here."

As usual, Rafiq began his restless pacing. "Are you saying I should return to the palace?"

"Not necessarily, Rafiq," Zain said. "Madison also informed the press that following your information-gathering, you would be taking a brief sabbatical."

Maysa could see several problems with that plan. "Are you certain that's a good idea with the media already making assumptions?"

Zain wrapped an arm around his wife's shoulder. "Madison and I both agree Rafiq still needs time away."

"But he can't stay here with you," Madison added. "He's going to have to find another place for his mini-vacation."

Rafiq stopped his pacing and stepped forward. "Would you please address me directly? And do not forget I have the ultimate decision whether I stay or go. If I decide to remain here, then that is what I will do."

Maysa looked directly at Rafiq for the first time since they'd received the news. "Madison's right, Rafiq.

You cannot remain here with me. The gossip will escalate, whether it's true or not."

"And that is the last thing you need right now," Zain said. "We are so close to having the council's full support for the water project. They need to know your complete focus is on your duty and not on a woman who…"

When Zain's words trailed off, Maysa's defenses went on high alert. "Whom they deem not worthy to wipe the king's feet?"

Madison reached over and patted Maysa's arm. "Believe me, I know exactly what you're going through, and I personally think the mores are ridiculous and archaic."

"This is not the time to try to change customs," Rafiq said. "It seems I have no other option than to lock myself in my suite and demand I not be disturbed."

"And that holds no guarantees you will not be disturbed," Zain added. "Should anyone learn you are there, the intrusions would continue. I suggest perhaps you leave the country. You could stay in our home in Los Angeles."

Rafiq released a caustic laugh. "If you recall, California is home to the press and paparazzi. I would be bothered there perhaps more than I would here. And I refuse to be so far away should an emergency arise."

"He's right," Madison said. "It would be best if we find a remote location near Bajul."

"He can stay at the resort." Maysa's abrupt, and somewhat loud, declaration had the effect of a gunshot. All eyes turned to her.

Madison appeared totally unimpressed by the suggestion. "I don't consider staying in a resort full of tourists as the best place to relax and avoid publicity."

"No one is presently staying there," Maysa said. "The main hotel is currently closed for renovations, but the stand-alone villas on the far side of the property are available. They're a perfect hideaway."

"What about the staff?" Zain asked.

"Shamil gave them all a vacation. In fact, he requested I stop by from time to time to oversee the workers."

Rafiq frowned. "With no staff available, then I would be charged with preparing my own meals and laundering my own clothing?"

Heaven help him if he had to lift a royal finger to do menial chores. "Every villa is equipped with a full kitchen and normally a private chef. Since that isn't the case at the moment, I would be willing to see you have the proper meals and I can have my own staff do your laundry."

"This could definitely work." Madison pointed a finger at Maysa. "But you'd have to find a way to remain undetected. Zain's guards ran off a few reporters who were hanging around at the gate when we arrived. I assure you, they'll return as soon as we leave."

"I'll travel at night," she said. "The building crews will be gone by then, so the risk of anyone seeing me would be minimal."

When Rafiq failed to respond, Zain turned his attention to him. "Does this appeal to you at all, brother?"

Rafiq finally dropped into a chair and stretched his long legs before him, as if he'd settled in for the unforeseeable future. "I am thinking."

"Don't think too long," Madison said. "We have to

decide now, otherwise you'll be forced to return to the palace whether you're ready or not."

Rafiq remained silent a few moments before sending a quick glance at Maysa. "I will agree to the plan, as long as Maysa is also in agreement."

She saw no reason not to agree. He would have his time away, and she would have time away from him. If he had stayed under her roof, the temptation would have been too great. As it stood now, they would be better off keeping their distance from each other. She would simply deliver his meals and laundry, then leave. If only she truly believed it would be that simple. "I agree it's the best option."

"Excellent." Zain shot to his feet, held out his hands to his wife and pulled her up from the sofa. "Now if the two of you will excuse us, as soon as we return the guards to the palace, we have plans of our own."

Madison checked her watch. "And we only have a couple of hours before your children demand to be fed."

"That is why they invented bottles," Zain muttered.

Madison patted his cheek. "Patience, sweetie. The lake isn't going anywhere, and neither is the mountain."

"Are you planning to have more children?" Rafiq said, sounding somewhat appalled.

Madison's cheeks flushed. "Well, no, we're not. But then we weren't planning the last two."

Maysa couldn't help but laugh again. "Then I suggest you make certain you are prepared to battle the powers of *Mabruruk*. I have condoms available should you need them."

Zain winked at his wife. "Thank you for the offer, Maysa, but we have everything under control."

Madison sent him a smile. "We better. As much

as I love our babies, I'm not sure how well we could handle two more."

Maysa experienced a tiny bite of envy over the couple's obvious love for each other. A love that had encouraged a king to give up his throne for the unacceptable woman he adored. If only she could be so fortunate.

Shaking off the melancholy, she gestured toward the corridor. "Since I certainly do not wish to delay you further, I'll see you both to the door."

Rafiq didn't bother to stand. "Before the two of you leave, I would caution you both to take care. But if you wish to provide a diversion by swimming nude in the lake during the light of day, you have my blessing."

"We are married and I am no longer the king," Zain said. "The press is not interested in my life any longer. In fact, I can parade naked in the streets if I so desire without earning a second glance."

"I don't know about that," Madison added. "I've seen you naked and it's pretty impressive."

Zain grinned before continuing the lecture aimed at his brother. "On the other hand, you, Rafiq, *are* the king. You are expected to behave with a measure of decorum, so I suggest you avoid being naked anywhere other than the shower."

The warning was not lost on Maysa. "I will make certain he keeps his clothes on in public." Her tongue seemed determined to get her in trouble. "I'll see you to the door so you may get on with your day."

After a brief exchange of goodwill between the brothers, Maysa escorted Zain and Madison to the door while Rafiq stayed behind. "You can both rest assured that we will be on our best behavior."

"I trust you will," Zain said as he kissed her cheek. "Do not let him have the upper hand and order you around. Stand firm."

"I'll try my best, Zain, but you and I both know your brother. He's nothing if not stubborn and persistent." And persuasive.

Once Zain started toward the awaiting car, Madison took Maysa's hands into hers. "If that whole best intentions thing to avoid Rafiq's charms doesn't work out for you, just make sure you're discreet. And most important, don't go anywhere near that damn mountain."

With that, Madison hurried away to join her husband, leaving Maysa alone to ponder her options. She couldn't exactly avoid the mountain since it shadowed the resort, as it did most of the town. And she definitely couldn't avoid Rafiq's charms as she saw to his comfort. But she could—and she would—stand firm. At least she had work to occupy her time and her mind.

"Are you certain you have to work tomorrow?"

They'd barely made it into the villa's door before Rafiq posed the query that sounded like the prelude to a proposition. Maysa set one of the paper sacks containing supplies on the kitchen's black granite counter and began rifling through it. "I have to be at the clinic tomorrow. I have a full schedule."

Rafiq leaned around her and placed another sack next to hers. "Will you not consider staying with me tonight?"

Oh, she had considered it on the drive to the resort. She was considering it now when he rested his palm on her waist and she could feel the warmth of his hand through the dress's cotton fabric. But she still planned to give him an emphatic no. Eventually. Right then she chose to ignore the question and his touch. Or at least try.

"My chef prepared these pastries for your breakfast," she said as she pulled a metal tin from the bag. "She also provided a nice lunch that I'm sure you will enjoy."

She took said lunch, sidestepped Rafiq and placed it in the refrigerator. After she closed the door and turned around, she found Rafiq leaning back against the opposite counter, arms folded across his chest, his eyes looking as dark and intense as a midnight storm.

"I will make it worth your while if you stay with me tonight." His deep, sensual voice, as well as the promise in his words, went straight to Maysa's head like a glass of fine French champagne.

Stand firm...

Turning her back, she continued to unload the last of the supplies. "It's almost a half-hour drive to the clinic."

"I will have one of the guards drive you."

"I have my own vehicle, remember?"

"Yes, I remember. I also recall what we almost did in that vehicle, and our plans to finish what we had barely begun. Had my brother not arrived, we would still be in your bed, and I would be deep inside you."

Maysa fumbled the coffee canister on her way to placing it in the overhead cabinet. The container hit the countertop with a thump, landed on the bamboo floor and rolled behind her. She closed her eyes and cursed her clumsiness. She opened her eyes the minute she heard Rafiq come up behind her. He brushed against her back as he set the coffee in the cabinet with little effort.

Maysa's effort to avoid him began to wane. She ducked under his arm, strode to the adjacent dining room and began rearranging the artificial flowers in the vase set in the middle of the heavy wood table. "I have to admit Shamil did a good job modernizing the villas. With all the granite and stainless appliances, the place looks almost American. There is a nice private pool in the courtyard and…"

A persistent king pressed against her back, generating enough heat to fuel the six-burner stove. Rafiq rested his right hand on her waist and his left hand higher, where he grazed his thumb back and forth along the side of her breast. Then he swept her hair aside and whisked a series of soft, warm kisses along the side of her neck. She could ignore him. She could pretend to ignore her body's immediate reaction. Or she could simply enjoy the moment.

When she tipped her head back against his shoulder, he kissed the corner of her mouth, and without warning, he turned her around and set her atop the table.

A laugh of surprise slipped out of her gaping mouth. "Are you attempting to disarm me?"

He rested his hands on her thighs. "I am trying to persuade you allow me to resume what we began earlier today."

"We're in the kitchen."

He planted his palms on her knees. "We are in the dining room next to the kitchen."

She narrowed her eyes. "Are you having some sort of sexist fantasy about having your way with a woman in a domestic setting?"

"You are my fantasy, and I would like to have my way with you in any setting."

He punctuated his point by kissing her without mercy. So lost in his gentle yet complete exploration of her mouth, a few moments passed before Maysa realized Rafiq was working her dress up her thighs. When she tensed, he brought his lips to her ear.

"Trust me."

She did trust him, so much so she didn't launch into all the reasons why they shouldn't do this as he reached beneath the dress and clasped the band low at her hips. She didn't issue one protest when he began to lower her panties. In fact, she lifted her hips, allowing him to pull them down her legs to drop onto the floor. She didn't question why she was sitting on a table with her hem almost to her waist. She didn't care that she was exposed to Rafiq's eyes as he nudged her legs apart. She certainly didn't care when he formed his hand between her thighs.

She tipped her head against his and lowered her gaze to watch the patently erotic scene. Not once had she climaxed with her former husband, and she worried she might not be able to now. But this was Rafiq, the one and only man who had ever given her one—several—before the foreplay culminated into full-blown lovemaking. He knew exactly where to touch her, how much pressure to apply until she bordered on begging him to hurry. Yet he continued to take his time, measuring each stroke until her legs began to tremble. A sense of relief blended with the heady sensations when she experienced the impending release. She inadvertently dug her nails into Rafiq's shoulders as the orgasm began to build in intensity. She bit back the scream resulting from sheer pleasure, not pain. He captured her gasp with another kiss, moving his tongue in sync with the finger he had eased inside her.

As the final wave subsided, Maysa kept her head lowered and tried to hold the unexpected tears at bay, to no avail. She quickly swiped away the few that slipped free and hoped Rafiq didn't notice.

"Did I hurt you?"

The distress in his voice drew Maysa's gaze to his. "Not at all. I wasn't certain I could feel that way again."

He kissed her forehead so tenderly she almost sobbed. "I despise what that monster did to you, yet I knew he would never break you."

"No, he did not." But Rafiq could very well break her heart again.

He leaned over, swept her underwear from the floor and handed them to her. "Now get dressed, return home and try to have a good night's sleep."

She was stunned he hadn't made another attempt to convince her to stay. "What about you?"

"I will be fine until you are ready to take the final step."

Was she ready? A few moments ago she would have gladly followed him into the bedroom. But perhaps he was right. Perhaps she needed more time to weigh the consequences. "You heard what Zain and Madison said. We should not be entertaining thoughts of further intimacy under the circumstances."

He visually tracked her movements as she slipped her panties back into place. "No one would need to know, Maysa."

"But I would know, Rafiq. If we made love, and a reporter asked me about our relationship, the truth would be written on my face."

"All the more reason for you to take some time away from your practice."

If only it were that simple. "My entire day is booked tomorrow, morning until late afternoon."

"Say the word and I will have my personal physician treat patients in your stead."

"He doesn't know my patients. They rely on me. They know me."

Rafiq clasped her waist, lifted her up and set her on her feet. "Then see your patients and come to me tomorrow night."

The temptation to say yes lived strong in Maysa. Temptation had gotten her into trouble before. "I'll think about it."

"That is all I ask."

His agreement came much too swift. "Then you'll be fine should I decide to have one of your guards deliver your dinner while I remain home?"

"Of course."

He gave her a brief kiss with only a light graze of his tongue. Yet that was enough for her to reconsider.

Before she did, Maysa grabbed her bag and began backing to the door. "I will let you know if I decide to join you tomorrow night."

A slightly arrogant grin lifted the corners of his beautiful mouth. "And if you decide not to come to me, mark my words, I will eventually come to you."

Six

"You have one remaining patient, Dr. Barad."

Maysa leaned over the counter and frowned at Demetria Christos, the fiftysomething office manager, who normally ran the clinic's office like a ship's captain. Tonight the woman seemed as tightly wound as her salt-and-pepper curls. "You told me fifteen minutes ago the last patient had left, Demetria."

She began rapping the desk with a pen. "He's a walk-in. An American traveling through the region. He says he requires a complete physical, although he looked well to me. Very well indeed."

She could refuse treatment, but then again, he could actually afford to pay for the services. She could always use extra money for supplies and salaries. "Where is Jumanah?"

"She left a few minutes ago with her husband, before the man arrived."

And that meant Maysa would be without a nurse to assist. Not necessarily an issue, but it would delay the process if she had to handle the entire treatment herself. "Fine. But please lock the door and hang the closed sign."

"I have already done both."

"What room is he in?"

Demetria resumed her annoying pen tapping. "Room one."

Maysa pushed off the counter then turned when she came upon an idea. "I have a favor to ask. Would you mind having Paulos prepare his eggplant moussaka to go, please?" One of Rafiq's favorites during the time when they would eat together at the Greek restaurant. Now that she had the dinner situation solved, she had to tackle the other—whether she would personally deliver it or summon one of his guards.

She sent Maysa a suspicious look. "You do not like eggplant, Doctor."

A faux pas of the first order. "It's for a friend. Someone who's in Bajul for a visit."

"A man friend?"

A royally gorgeous man friend. "Yes, but he is nothing more than a casual acquaintance." And that was nothing less than a colossal lie.

Demetria looked crestfallen. "I am disappointed you have yet to find a suitable companion. Perhaps you would reconsider using my matchmaking talents?"

She would rather eat eggplant. "No, thank you, and feel free to go to the restaurant now."

"You want me to leave you alone with a stranger?"

The woman had a point. "Does he look threatening?"

"He is very tall and lean and quite handsome." She topped off the comment with a smitten smile.

Not the answer Maysa needed. "But does he appear to be the criminal sort?"

"My instincts say he is harmless, and my instincts are never wrong."

Except for the time Demetria had coerced her into a date with a local banker who was eight years' Maysa's junior and as interesting as a spreadsheet. "Then clearly there isn't any reason why you shouldn't leave."

"This is true. His chart is on the door."

"Thank you, and I'll be by to pick up my order as soon as I'm finished here." Maysa spun around and headed down the tiled hallway, exhaustion weighting her steps. She grabbed the chart from the holder and scanned the intake form only containing his last name as she entered the room. "What can I do for you, Mr. King?"

"I am open to all suggestions."

She glanced up from the page to see Rafiq casually perched on the edge of the exam table, one leg slightly bent, one foot planted on the floor. He wore a tailored white shirt, black dress slacks and an expression that said he was greatly enjoying his little surprise.

"What are you doing here?" she asked as soon as she found her voice.

"As I told your secretary, I am here for a complete physical."

That came as no real surprise. "You have your own physician."

"He is not presently available."

As if she believed that. "Did Demetria recognize you?"

"She did, but I asked her not to tell you."

That certainly explained the office manager's odd behavior, yet it did not explain Rafiq's lack of wisdom. "Do you realize the risk you took coming here? Anyone could have seen your armored car and—"

"I walked from the palace," he said. "I had the guards deliver me there and then set out on foot. That served as a sufficient decoy."

"Since it's at least a mile from the palace to the clinic, obviously you're not in dire straits as far as your physical health is concerned." She would have to question his mental health for walking the streets in broad daylight.

He leveled his dark gaze directly on hers. "I do have an ache that does not seem to want to go away."

She decided to play along, probably at her own detriment. "Where exactly is this ache?"

"I will show you."

When Rafiq slid off the table and began unbuckling his belt, Maysa pointed at him. "Do not remove one article of clothing, Your Majesty."

He had the gall to grin. "Then how will you treat this ache if you do not see its origin?"

Do not humor him, Maysa. She smiled in spite of herself. "Believe me, I don't have to see it to know how to diagnose it. It could possibly be priapism, although that usually occurs when the erection remains long after sexual intercourse."

"I see." He rubbed his shadowed jaw and studied the ceiling before returning his attention to her. "Then how do I find relief, Doctor?"

She tossed the chart onto the counter housing the sink. "I don't believe the answer to that requires my expertise. However, I do require an answer from you. Once again, why are you here?"

He took two slow steps toward her. "I am here to ask if you will be coming tonight."

If he had his way, she would be—in every respect. "It's been less than twenty-four hours since you asked, and I still have not decided."

He moved as close as he could, pinning Maysa against the counter, his hands braced on either side of her. "Is there something I could do to persuade you?"

The images from the dining table incident filtered into her muddled mind. The feelings of absolute desire were still fresh, and threatening to reappear. "Give me more time, and some space."

He straightened and slid his hands into his pockets. "I will not pressure you to make a decision, yet I will be disappointed if you leave me to while away the hours all alone, with no relief for my condition… What is it called?"

"Priapism, and you don't actually have it. You do have the means to relieve it by taking matters into your own hands."

That earned her another one of his deadly smiles. "And what would be the pleasure in that when you could take matters into your hands?"

Maysa was growing very hot, and very bothered. "I suggest you go back to the villa and await my decision like a good little king."

"How will I know what that decision will be?"

"When you see me at the doorstep. Or not."

"Then I will wait all night if I must." His expression turned suddenly serious. "Before I leave, I need you to know I understand your hesitancy, and the reason behind it. You fear the loss of control."

Rafiq had definitely hit the mark with that assumption. "You're right. Losing control is something I no longer take lightly."

"You might also believe I am being selfish." He released a rough sigh. "Perhaps I am. Yet I have learned that life holds no assurances, and the time we have is relatively short-lived. But at the moment, time together is all we have, no matter how brief."

And brief it would be. Once this affair was over, should it actually begin in earnest, they would go back to leading separate lives, as they had been for well over a decade.

He took her hands, turned them over and placed a tender kiss above the scar on one wrist, then the other. "If you decide to join me tonight, I will promise to give you my complete attention, and I will allow you all the control."

He then strode out the door, while Maysa remained in the room to mull over his vow. Rafiq Mehdi wasn't the kind of man to give up control under any circumstance. He was still the man she'd known long ago—an abiding tenderness existed beneath the steel exterior. He'd demonstrated that only moments ago. Would it be worth the risk to her emotional health if she made love with him again? Could she walk away as if nothing had ever existed between them?

She had traveled down that treacherous road before, and she had survived. She would definitely survive this time.

Maysa Barad would never allow any man—not even the man she had always loved—to break her again.

* * *

Rafiq had constantly been decisive when it came to duty. When it involved lovemaking, he was much the same. He had always taken the lead after making the first move. To relinquish that power would be completely foreign to him, yet he would for Maysa—provided she finally arrived.

She had phoned a half hour ago to inform him she was on her way. He had walked the floor as he'd waited, wondering if perhaps she had changed her mind. In accordance with his plan, he wore only a robe and nothing else. A distinct risk, but he had a point to prove. He also had a tenuous hold on his libido when he heard the lock trip.

Maysa entered the front door carrying a brown paper sack. She stopped short the moment her gaze fell on where he now stood, attempting to affect a calm he did not remotely feel.

She clutched the bag tighter and cleared her throat. "Obviously you've run out of clean clothes."

"I still have a surplus. I decided to wait to shower until after your arrival."

The discomfort in her expression indicated she understood what he was proposing. "I brought dinner from the Greek restaurant."

The low-cut yellow gauze dress she wore almost brought him to his knees. "Would you be dining with me?"

She shook her head. "No. I had a late lunch."

"As did I. You may put it away and I will reheat it later in the microwave."

"You know how to use the microwave?"

"I have two graduate degrees. I believe I can find

which button to press." He had one particular button in mind, but it would not be found in the kitchen.

"Far be it for me to force you to eat," she said. "I'll put this in the refrigerator."

"And I will retire to the shower." Without formality or fair warning, Rafiq removed the robe and set it aside on the sofa. "You are welcome to join me."

He expected Maysa to protest his boldness or perhaps leave out the door. Instead, she took a slow visual voyage down his body. He reacted as any man would, particularly a man in the presence of a woman he wanted with a fierceness unlike any he had known.

Her eyes widened slightly when she arrived at the destination that heralded the obvious results of her perusal. "I see your condition hasn't improved."

"It still requires treatment. After your hectic day, are you up for a further examination?"

"You are clearly up for it." She raised her gaze and smiled, presenting her dimples as one more weapon in her female arsenal. "I might be persuaded to lend a hand in a while. In the meantime, I suggest you retire to the shower."

"And you will join me?" He was quite surprised by the eagerness in his voice, and evidently so was Maysa.

"Perhaps, but first I must return a phone call from a patient."

Her profession seemed destined to intrude on their time. "Will this require you to make a home visit?"

"I won't know until I speak with him."

He inclined his head and narrowed his eyes. "Is this truly a patient, or a secret lover?"

She rolled her eyes. "It's a seventy-year-old farmer with a cold. I highly doubt his wife of fifty years would approve of me taking him as a lover. Besides, one lover at a time is all I can handle."

The promise in her words and her eyes lifted Rafiq's spirits. "Then I shall be in the shower, awaiting your care."

Gathering his strength, Rafiq turned away from Maysa, though he sincerely wanted to take her down on the sofa and dispense with further delay, as well as her clothing. He crossed the expansive master bedroom and entered the bath that was truly fit for a king. The stone shower was equally large, perhaps large enough for five people, and well appointed. He depressed the control on the wall that slid the ceiling open to reveal open air and a host of stars. He then set the temperature and started the water for two of the four showerheads.

After stepping beneath the spray, he braced both hands on the tiled walls and attempted to regain some control. If he failed, Maysa's examination would be over before it had begun. *If* she had not decided to take up with the farmer and leave him behind. He decided to bathe and hope for the best.

When several minutes had passed, and he was thoroughly clean and somewhat composed, he began to believe Maysa had changed her mind. Perhaps she had...

"The doctor has arrived."

The sound of her voice drew his attention to the shower's opening. The sight of her standing there, without any clothing and seemingly relaxed, shattered his calm into a million shards of human glass. He had never seen Maysa completely nude, even in their youth when their covert meetings had been conducted in darkness. The golden cast of the overhead light illuminated each detail, from the fullness of her breasts capped with light brown nipples, the indentation of her waist, the curve of her hips and the shading between her thighs.

When she stepped into the shower, he grew painfully hard and extremely aware that he would have to develop superhuman strength in the next few moments.

Maysa moved beneath the spray opposite him and closed her eyes as the water flowed over her. After Rafiq pushed aside the showerhead above him to gain a better view, his anticipation heightened while he watched her bathe. He followed the movement of her hands as she washed her breasts, then her abdomen and lower still. He wanted to go to her, touch her, kiss the moisture from her body one blessed inch at a time. Yet he had promised to relinquish his control. Therefore he had no choice but to wait until she came to him.

She rinsed the soap from her body, slicked back her long hair and finally approached him. But when he reached for her, she took a step back. "Before we continue, I need to outline some rules."

He could not conceal his frustration. "More rules?"

"For now," she said. "First, do not touch me until I give you permission."

"That is not acceptable—"

She held up a hand to silence him. "Don't forget that I am in control, as you ordained."

He had not forgotten, though he had begun to regret it. "Continue."

"Next, you cannot kiss me, at least for the time being."

He was quickly taking exception to her rules, yet he knew better than to argue. "All right. Is there anything else I might do to accommodate you?"

"Yes." She closed the space between them and reached up to move the spray over them. "Enjoy being stripped of your control."

Her eyes seemed alight with fire as she placed her hands on his chest, pausing to touch his nipples with deft fingertips. He sucked in a deep breath when she drew a path down his belly. He clenched his jaw tightly when she circled his navel, and tighter still when she raked her nails lightly down his thighs.

She seemed to be purposefully avoiding his erection, or perhaps bent on torturing him until he begged her. She undeniably had torture in mind, he realized, when she lowered herself onto her knees. The minute she took him into her mouth, he began the battle to remain in control of his body, the only control he still retained.

When she used her tongue like a feather, from tip to shaft, Rafiq focused on trivial details in an effort to prolong the experience—his least favorite foods, his agenda for the next council meeting, the extreme heat in August. He even attempted to recall the words to the Petrarca poem Elena had forced him to memorize. Nothing worked as a sufficient distraction, until he ventured a glance at Maysa kneeling before him. Seeing her there, appearing subservient, gave him pause, as well as a temporary respite from the need for gratification.

He broke a rule by lifting her to her feet, immediately earning him a look of displeasure. "Did I do something wrong?" she asked, sounding unsure.

"You were doing everything right, and it took great effort for me to stop you."

"Then why did you?"

"Because you should never be on your knees before any man." Least of all him—a man who could give her nothing more than temporary pleasure.

"But you didn't force me on my knees, Rafiq. There is a difference."

"Still, I wish to see your eyes when you touch me."

Her smile reappeared, soft and sensual. "Let's see how long you can keep them open when I continue."

And continue she did, using her hands as effectively as she had her mouth. She increased the cadence of her strokes, making it difficult for Rafiq to draw a breath, or to keep his eyes open. In a matter of moments, he would lose both the battle and the war. He would lose the opportunity to carry her to the bed and bury himself inside her.

"Stop." The demand echoed in the shower like a gunshot.

"No," she replied, then sent a pointed look at his hand circling her wrist.

He reluctantly released her and prepared to plead his case. "If you continue, I am in grave danger of—"

"I know. That is my intention."

She had turned the tables on him, implementing her own plan that would surely drive him to the brink of pleasurable insanity. Yet she was empowered, and he was powerless. Powerless to stop her determined, thorough touching. Powerless to hold out any longer when she brought her lips to his ear and whispered, "Be grateful you are surrendering your control to a physician."

And without warning, she pressed her free hand between his legs at the same time the climax crashed down on him with the force of an explosion. He tipped his head back against the wall as a harsh, guttural moan slipped out of his mouth. The orgasm continued longer than any he had experienced before, and the impact almost buckled his knees. By the time the sensations began to wane, he realized his heart was beating dangerously fast.

He finally opened his eyes to Maysa, who seemed very proud of her accomplishment. "What did you do to me?" he grated out.

She streamed a fingertip along his jaw. "Aside from giving you the most intense orgasm you've ever experienced?"

"*How* did you do it?"

"I happen to know a certain trigger point that reportedly increases a man's pleasure. I've never tried it before, but I assume it worked."

"Had it worked any better, I would be dead."

She laid her cheek on the left side of his chest before returning her gaze back to his. "Your heart is still beating strongly, so I do believe you will live."

"For a moment I was in doubt." And in less than a moment, he would kiss her, damn the rules.

"I'm certain you have no doubts about one particular aspect of the experience."

"What would that be?"

Her expression turned from amused to sultry. "Isn't handing your control to a woman a complete rush?"

And now the time had come to reclaim that control.

He spun her around against the wall, framed her face in his palms and kissed her without hesitation, using his tongue to simulate the act of lovemaking that he planned to undertake tonight. He would need time to recover, but he knew exactly what to do with that time.

He broke the kiss but kept hold of her face. "You do not have the market cornered on your so-called trigger points. I know where they exist on you, and I intend to explore each and every one, perhaps more than once."

"But—"

He pressed a finger to her lips. "This is my plan, and these are my rules. I expect you to touch me, and I will be kissing you often. Everywhere. Do you understand?"

She appeared as if she might respond but nodded instead.

"Good. Now before I carry you to bed, I have one last remark."

"Please do, but hurry." Her words came out in a raspy whisper.

"If you trust me enough to give up your control to me, I will give you an experience you will not soon forget."

Seven

Maysa wouldn't soon forget the expectation in Rafiq's dark eyes as he awaited her answer. If she agreed to his request, she would acknowledge that she was finally ready for that next all-important step—letting go and letting him make love to her in every possible way, and the possibilities were endless. She wanted to experience each and every one with him. She needed to forget the horror her life had been with Boutros. Rafiq alone could erase those memories from her mind with only a kiss.

She took both his hands into hers. "I trust you, Rafiq. Do with me what you will, as long as you do it very, very soon."

When he swept her up into his arms, Maysa laughed from surprise and a sheer sense of freedom. She continued to laugh as he strode into the bedroom and deposited her on the edge of the mattress. She stopped laughing when he stood before her, his golden skin and thick dark hair still damp from their water play, arms dangling at his sides, every astounding inch of him exposed to her eyes. One prime, naked, beautiful male. All hers to enjoy with touches and kisses. Definitely kisses, and she craved one now.

She turned her focus on his mouth and made a rather ridiculous observation in light of their current situation. "You shaved again."

He rubbed a hand over his jaw. "Yes, and with good reason. As you've said, women at times find facial hair irritating. I would not want that for you."

"I like you better without the goatee."

"I am pleased you are pleased."

Maysa would be more pleased if he would make some move to touch or kiss her. Anything to put her out of her misery. After the shower escapade, she was so sexually keyed up she could jump out of her skin, or jump all over him.

Yet he continued to survey her as if intentionally prolonging her agony. "Rafiq, are you simply going to stand there all night and assess me?"

"No." He leaned forward and planted his palms on either side of her hips. "I am trying to decide exactly what I wish to do with you."

"I don't care. Just do it."

He barked out a laugh. "Patience has never been one of your virtues, but since I am now in control, you will have to find some."

She sighed. "You're frustrating me so much I want to scream."

He gave her a wry grin. "I assure you, screaming

could very well be involved. Or at the very least, moaning."

His words blanketed her body with another round of heat. His sudden, deep kiss landed that heat right between her thighs. After he had kissed her quite thoroughly, he began a trek down her body with his lips, pausing at her breasts to pay each equal attention with the tip of his tongue and the steady pull of his mouth.

When she tried to take him back onto the bed, he rejected her efforts and straightened. "Patience," he reminded her. "I want you to remain where I have placed you."

He wanted her to continue to sit up? "What if I want to lie back?"

"I will inform you when that is permissible."

He was beginning to take the power play to the extreme, but who was she to question him? She had stripped him of all control in the shower, and seeing him that helpless had been a complete and utter turn-on. "Your wish is my command, Sayyed."

"And my command is that you take pleasure in the experience," he said, tossing her words back at her.

"I'm sure I will, as soon as you give it to me."

"I have every intention of giving it to you." When he raked his gaze down her body and back up again, she literally squirmed. "Do you know what you deserve?" he asked.

A medal for remaining upright. "No, what do I deserve?"

He leaned forward again and kissed her lightly. "A man who is willing—" he lowered himself to the floor "—to fall to his knees before you."

His tender words and actions shot straight to Maysa's heart. "I don't know what to say."

"Say nothing," he said. "Only feel."

When he parted her legs, Maysa trembled from anticipation. She became keenly aware that he was about to undertake what no man had ever dared. She had been with two men—and the one before her had never attempted this. The other had only been concerned with his own sadistic gratification, not hers.

Still, she wasn't a child. She knew all there was to know about human sexuality and female anatomy. But she had no personal barometer with which to measure how this ultimate intimacy would feel. She would soon find out, she realized, as Rafiq slid his hands beneath her bottom and kissed his way up her inner thighs.

The minute he reached the intended target, she acknowledged he had a wonderfully wicked mouth, and he used it on her with the skill of a man experienced in the art of lovemaking. As she witnessed the act, she had trouble catching her breath, but couldn't. With every pass of his tongue, she tried very hard to take in all the sensations, but she was beginning to enter the realm where thought was impossible. Her hips involuntarily tilted toward him, prompting Rafiq to be even more deliberate. And that in turn brought about a climax that jarred her like an unpredictable bolt of lightning.

The impact left her weak and winded and momentarily incoherent from the wonder of it all. But she wasn't so mentally jumbled that she didn't notice the typical male pride in Rafiq's expression as he rested his chin on her shaky knees.

"That was quick," she said when she'd recovered enough to speak. "And totally amazing."

"I agree it was over too quickly for you to enjoy the full effect. It will not be that way the second time."

Surely he didn't mean… Oh, yes, he did. "Rafiq, I can't…"

"Do not underestimate yourself," he said. "Or me."

Multiple orgasms had never been a part of her limited sexual repertoire. She knew they were possible, but could she truly hope they were possible for her? She sought confirmation as Rafiq went back to his ministrations, this time using his hand as well as his mouth. She remained more aware of what he was doing this time, but no less excited to have him do it. No less in need of a release. The climax began to gain momentum, more tempered this time, but still potent. And when Rafiq hit her "trigger spot," the orgasm caused her to curl over his head to anchor herself.

Maysa fell back on the bed, closed her eyes and waited for the endless tremors to subside, willing her pulse to steady. Only a few moments passed before she felt the mattress bend beside her.

"Are you all right?"

She opened her eyes and focused on that remarkable, endearing smile. "I have traveled to that state known as euphoria."

His deep laugh gave her the chills all over again. "I believe I visited there in the shower."

"I never knew," she said, struggling to express what she was feeling.

"Never knew what?"

She rolled toward him and touched his face. "I never knew I could feel so much. I truly did believe Boutros had destroyed all that was good about lovemaking. I have you to thank for helping me to see it can be good. Better than good."

He pushed her damp hair back and kissed her forehead. "You are not required to thank me, and the best is yet to come. If you are ready."

How could she not be? "I am more than ready, and weary of waiting."

"Good. Get dressed."

She had not expected that perplexing order. "Is this some new technique you've learned, making love fully clothed?"

"No. I want to take you somewhere special to make love to you."

He was certainly full of surprises tonight. "Where would that be?"

"Our past."

If only they could actually return to those carefree days. If only they could change the course of their history and the confines of their culture. If only they had found some way to be together permanently.

Maysa dealt daily in reality, not impossibilities. Time could not be rewound, and even if it could, she wasn't certain she would turn back the clock. Every heartbreak, every moment of torture, had driven her to succeed. Every disappointment had made her who she was today—a strong, independent woman. A physician. If she had been chosen to be Rafiq's wife, she would have eventually been relegated to entertain dignitaries and churn out royal heirs. She had always wanted to be a doctor, and she probably would not have been allowed the opportunity had she married Rafiq. Resentment might have destroyed their love.

Nevertheless, the past was dead and buried, and the present was all that mattered right now. She would concentrate on that as they set off on their mystery journey.

Yet the mystery ended the moment Rafiq steered the Hummer off the main highway and Maysa realized exactly where they were going—their secret sanctuary.

Ancient olive trees lined the narrow lane, welcoming them back to the large parcel of Mehdi-owned land that bordered the palace grounds. The private grove where she and Rafiq had come of age in each other's arms. Where they had first declared their love, all the while knowing that love would never be enough to sustain their relationship. Not when culture and customs had intruded.

As pavement turned to gravel, Maysa powered down the window, allowing the warm breeze to reintroduce her to the scents and sounds of nature in its purest form. Rafiq pulled between two acacia trees adjacent to the small clearing that had served as their special meeting place. He shut off the ignition and left on the parking lights that illuminated the tufts of grass and aloe plants in a golden glow.

After taking in the sight, she shifted slightly toward Rafiq. "It looks the same as it did before. I do hope the caretaker still keeps the wolves away."

He draped an arm over the steering wheel and stared out the windshield. "No one has spotted a wolf in a number of years."

That gave her only a small measure of comfort. "I suppose we could have brought along one of your guards, although having an audience would be rather awkward."

"They are positioned on the main road in front of the entrance to the property."

Wonderful. "They're not going to be patrolling the area, are they?"

"They will remain in the car, as I have instructed. We will not be disturbed."

"Good. I'd hate to be caught—"

"Naked?" He accentuated the comment with a sensual grin.

"Exactly."

"I will protect you from prying eyes if necessary."

She smiled at a sudden recollection. "If my memory serves me correctly, you insisted on coming to my bed that first time because you worried someone would catch us here without our clothes. Now you're suggesting we take off all our clothes here and the threat is still real."

He reached across the console and took her hand. "With age and experience comes the need for adventure."

"As long as that adventure does not include ants and other creatures of the night."

He brought her face around and kissed her. "I will protect you from all predators."

Maysa fished two condoms from the side pocket of her casual dress and prepared for Rafiq's reaction. "And I am in charge of protecting us from pregnancy."

As she'd predicted, he scowled. "Although I understand the necessity, I am not pleased with having a barrier between us."

"A thin barrier. You'll barely know it's there."

"I will know, and why only two?"

She slapped playfully at his arm with the back of

her hand. "I have a whole box at the resort if this is not enough."

"That is good to know." He reached behind the seat and brought out two of the hotel's blankets. "Now it is time to put these barriers to good use."

Maysa waited while Rafiq rounded the Hummer and opened her door. After he took her hand to help her out, they walked, arms around waists, toward the far side of the field that contained more sand than foliage.

Rafiq let Maysa go to spread out one of the blankets, then dropped the other on the ground beside the pallet. "In case we need to cover ourselves should we be visited by an intruder."

She truly hoped that wouldn't be necessary. "Well?" she asked when neither made a move to undress.

"Shoes first," he said as he lowered onto the blanket and began removing his boots.

Maysa slipped off her sandals while Rafiq stripped out of his shirt. Although the light was limited to a three-quarter moon, she could still make out his body's finer details—the webwork of masculine veins in his strong arms, the bulk of his biceps and the ridged plane of his belly. She had seen those details earlier, among others, yet she found she would gladly study them for hours. She also discovered a sense of daring that had been missing from her life for several years.

After she stepped onto the edge of the blanket, she pitched the condoms to Rafiq, who made a perfect one-handed catch. She reached behind her, slid the back zipper down and then lowered the straps. She let the dress fall in a pool of gauze at her feet, drawing Rafiq's attention to her bare breasts. When she shimmied out of her panties and kicked them aside, he released an audible groan.

"Have I told you how beautiful you are?" he asked, his voice noticeably strained as he lowered his fly.

She didn't need to hear the compliment—she could see the appreciation in his eyes, and elsewhere when he had dispensed with the rest of his clothes. And she had no qualms about taking a long look elsewhere. "Thank you, Your Highness. I feel the same about you." She felt so much for him that her emotions were heading into a tailspin.

Rafiq patted the space beside him. "If you are ready to proceed, join me."

Deciding to take that daring for another spin, Maysa went to her knees, crawled toward him and reached over to retrieve one discarded packet. After withdrawing the condom, she nudged Rafiq onto his back and took the liberty of rolling it into place, with a few added unnecessary adjustments for good measure.

She then stretched out atop the length of him. "I believe I've proven I am more than ready." She shimmied her hips against him. "So are you."

With one smooth move, he flipped her onto her back. She expected to see amusement in his eyes, but instead, she saw worry. "Again, if you wish me to stop, say so. If you experience any pain, tell me."

She loved him for his concern. She loved him for more reasons than she could count. "I'm positive that will not happen. After all, this is what we've been waiting for, and I trust you'll make it worth the wait."

He lifted her chin and kissed her briefly. "I will do everything in my power to make it right for you."

"And you are a very powerful man, Rafiq Mehdi, oh, king of the female climax."

Finally, his smile reappeared. "I will endeavor to continue to earn that title, beginning now."

And he did, without a moment's hesitation. After a few expert touches and one long, hot kiss, he quickly took her to the brink and she was on the verge of pleading and promising him anything if he would take her all the way. Then he removed his hand, raised slightly, moved over her.

Maysa braced for the inevitable, so certain she could handle the culmination of all their foreplay. Yet when he began to ease inside her, her body tensed even though her mind told her this was not an invasion. This was Rafiq, the man she trusted with her life.

Rafiq stilled and responded by uncurling her fisted hands and kissing her palms. He then began speaking to her in Arabic. Soft words. Sensuous words. Descriptive words that painted a picture of how she felt surrounding him. How he had waited a lifetime to be this close to her again. How his greatest desire was to give her the utmost pleasure.

Before Maysa realized it, they were completely joined; she was entirely free of any resistance and once more caught in the throes of an orgasm the moment he began to move. As the cadence of his thrusts increased, she smoothed her hands over his back, memorized every nuance, reveled in his power and remembered that one night when she had given herself to him the first time. When she had willingly handed over her heart, only to have it shattered by his duty. And it would invariably happen again if she allowed it.

She refused to consider that now. She only wanted

to concentrate on these precious moments when nothing mattered but making love with him. Loving him.

After Rafiq collapsed against her with a low moan, Maysa's unwanted tears again broke through despite her determination not to cry in front of him for the second time in as many days. The emotional fortress she had erected for self-protection had begun to crumble in his presence.

"Once more, I have brought you to tears, and I am sorry for that."

Maysa opened her eyes and tried to smile, a shaky one. "These special moments made me cry, Rafiq. Not you. They're good tears."

"I have never known tears to be good."

Spoken like a man who probably hadn't cried since childhood. "Sometimes they're necessary. An emotional release of sorts. You don't need to worry."

He brushed a damp strand of hair away from her cheek. "Yet I do worry. I worry about what will happen after we part ways again."

So was she. "Let's not ruin this by talking about that. We still have time. Tomorrow is Saturday, which means I have nowhere I need to be."

"I need to be with you," he said. "The entire weekend. I do not want to be away from you for even an hour."

"Then I am yours." For the weekend. Beyond that, who knew?

He brought her against his chest and rubbed her arm in a soothing rhythm. "Perhaps we should begin our time together in a real bed."

Maysa smiled in earnest. "I agree. I think I'm lying on a tree root, or perhaps a tortoise."

He shifted to where they faced each other. "Shall we drive back naked?"

"Oh, no, let's walk back naked. If we're lucky, we'll stumble upon some hapless reporter and provide a story that will span the ages. I can see it now—King Rafiq Mehdi Plays Doctor with Local Doctor."

Their shared laughter echoed over the olive grove, drowning out the night sounds and the inevitable goodbye hanging over them like a guillotine. Maysa wanted more laughter in the time they had left. She would reserve the tears for after he was gone.

Rafiq could not recall a time when he had been consumed by such fierce emotion. As Maysa slept in his arms, he held her as tightly as he dared for fear of rousing her. She needed rest as much as he needed her. He planned to wake her in the morning with kisses and make love to her most of the day. Lose himself in her for as long as possible, until he was forced to leave her behind again. Forced to find a more suitable woman in the eyes of the elders and the country at large. He knew no woman who would be as suitable for him as Maysa. But he would not subject her to the cruelty he inherently knew would exist if he took her as his future queen. He would not risk failing another woman.

Oddly, the guilt over his role in Rima's death had subsided over the past few days, yet it once more reared its ugly head. He had selfishly and willingly drawn Maysa into this doomed affair, and now he would suffer the consequences of his actions by losing her a second time.

Before that happened, he had much he needed to tell her, including all that had transpired the night of

Rima's death. Perhaps then Maysa would understand why he did not deserve her devotion. Perhaps then their parting would be easier. Swift and sure, as it should be. Once he confessed, she would not look upon him the same way. She would not be able to forgive him, as he had not been able to forgive himself.

In the interim, he would cherish this fleeting fantasy they had created, and he would show Maysa the depth of his feelings by giving her his undivided attention. He dared not put those feelings into words, for to declare them out loud would only wound her further.

Yet as he gazed upon her beautiful face and saw the girl she had been, as well as the remarkable woman she had become, he whispered those words without thought. With the reverence of a prayer.

"Ana bahebik."

I love you....

Eight

Maysa had always looked forward to Monday mornings, a day when she could leave the boring weekend behind to face the challenges of her profession. Today, with a remarkable man sleeping soundly at her side, she hated Monday.

In a little over an hour, she would reluctantly leave Rafiq to go work after spending a weekend with him that had been anything but uneventful. On the contrary, she'd experienced the best two days of her life to this point. She'd become someone unrecognizable to herself, a woman transformed into a high-voltage mass of sexual energy. She and Rafiq had made love in many different ways, and in many different places. She had done things with him that she'd never dreamed she would do, and the rewards had been phenomenal. He'd guided her into a paradise built on experimentation and a total loss of inhibition. They'd foregone clothing for easy access whenever the lovemaking mood struck them, and it had quite often.

But during the aftermath, when they'd been temporarily satisfied to only hold each other, they talked about times gone by and the road to her career. They'd discussed world politics and Rafiq's role in Bajul's future. They had covered everything but their impending goodbye.

Maysa had been grateful for that. She preferred to focus on the present and quiet, unforgettable moments such as this. She propped up on one elbow, supported her cheek with her palm and took the opportunity to study Rafiq, now stretched out on his back. He had a perfectly sculpted profile, as did all the Mehdi sons, only one of the reasons their photos had been in high demand and plastered all over the internet. Extraordinarily beautiful men with political power and untold wealth. The pinnacle of masculinity in a package of three.

But right now, with his eyes closed and his features slack, Rafiq looked more teenage boy than adult monarch to Maysa. More innocent than experienced. The motherless child who had strived to be worthy of his father's respect. The king of her damaged heart.

When he began to stir, she smoothed a wayward lock of hair back and kissed his forehead. His eyes opened slowly, followed by a patently sensual smile. The adult Rafiq had returned.

"I am surprised you are awake," he said in a sexy morning voice.

"I have to go into the clinic in a bit."

He turned toward her and outlined her lips with a

fingertip. "Can I persuade you to take another day off to spend with me?"

He could, if she let him, but she wouldn't. "This is my life, Rafiq, taking care of people. I have a responsibility to my patients to show up and…"

Her words trailed off the minute Rafiq's hand landed on her breast. She should move it immediately, before he moved that hand significantly lower. But as he began that predictable downward trek, his cell began to ring, momentarily keeping Maysa from throwing caution and obligation to the desert winds.

Rafiq fell back against the pillow, snatched the offending phone from the nightstand and answered with a gruff, "What do you want, Zain?"

Maysa settled her head on his shoulder, her palm resting on his sternum. She listened to the steady beat of his heart, as well as the one-sided conversation that seemed somewhat tense.

"I will be preoccupied for the next hour," he said. "But you may call after that if any issue arises."

Then out of the blue, Rafiq guided Maysa's hand beneath the sheet to show her exactly what had arisen. She attempted to ignore his personal "issue," not by taking her hand away, but by leaving it still.

Rafiq caught her gaze, smiled and winked at her before he continued. "I trust you can handle it." Maysa stifled a laugh when he added, "No, I was not speaking to you, Zain," followed by a long pause when Maysa could no longer resist the temptation to drive him crazy with a few practiced touches.

"What am I doing at the moment?" Rafiq drew in a broken breath and let it out slowly. "I am considering a long morning ride. I will see you this afternoon."

After he hung up, Rafiq immediately tossed the phone aside, while Maysa threw back the covers. After that, everything happened very quickly—fumbling for a condom, touching with abandon, making love as if tomorrow would not arrive. After the frantic session was over, they remained in each other's arms while their bodies calmed and their breathing returned to normal.

Yes, these were the moments she appreciated the most. She would take them to memory and bring them out when they were all she had left of him.

The shrill of the alarm forced Maysa out of the fantasy world and back into reality. She reluctantly left him and sat up. "I have to get ready for work." When Rafiq didn't respond, she glanced to her right to find him staring at the ceiling. "Is something wrong?"

"A complication with one of the council members," he said without looking at her. "I must return to the palace this afternoon."

"Permanently?" She despised the disappointment in her voice, but she wasn't prepared for their parting.

"I am not certain," he said. "It will depend on the outcome of the meeting."

She rose from the bed, grabbed the robe from the nearby chair and slipped it on. "I hope it goes well."

"As do I."

On the chance this could be the final time they would be together alone, she decided to make an offer he wouldn't refuse. "I'm going to shower now. Would you like to join me?"

He moved up against the wood headboard and raked both hands through his hair. "I will shower in the secondary bath. After you are dressed, meet me in the living area. We have a few things to discuss."

A strong sense of dread shot all the way to her soul. "All right. I will see you in a while."

As she bathed, Maysa tried to tell herself this could only have to do with Rafiq's duty, and not their relationship. She had little luck in convincing herself that was the truth. By the time she was finished dressing and out the bedroom door, she was resigned to hearing goodbye.

When she entered the living room, Maysa discovered Rafiq leaning forward on the edge of the small divan, his head lowered and his hands laced together between his knees. When he looked up, she immediately noticed the weariness in his eyes.

She swallowed around the knot in her throat and took the space beside him. "I am fairly certain I know what you are about to say."

He sighed and leaned back against the magenta cushion. "You have no way of knowing what I am about to say until after I say it. And once the words leave my mouth, you will never view me in the same light again."

She clasped his hand to reassure him that nothing he said would ever change her mind about him. "Rafiq, we've both known our time together would eventually come to an end sooner than later."

"You misunderstand," he said. "This is not about us."

Now she was sincerely confused. "Did something happen at the palace in your absence?"

"No. I need to tell you what transpired the night Rima died. I have been carrying the burden far too long."

Relief washed over her, though she was still concerned. "Go ahead. I'm listening."

He hesitated a few moments before he continued. "Shortly after dinner that evening, she came into my study and told me of the pregnancy. I was pleased with the news and hopeful that having a child together would restore our civility, if not our friendship. She did not agree."

"Then she wasn't even the least bit happy about the baby?" Maysa asked, though she had seen indications of that unhappiness when Rima had come to her for confirmation.

"No, she was not happy. I requested we make a formal announcement, yet she refused. She said she did not want anyone to know until she was more than two weeks along in the pregnancy."

Warning bells rang out in Maysa's head. "Are you certain she wasn't further along?"

"I am certain. Why would you believe otherwise?"

She had no one to blame but herself for walking into this snake pit. Still, she was trapped between upholding patient confidentiality and being up front with Rafiq. She chose the former for the time being. "I apologize. You were her husband and you would most likely know when she conceived."

"I knew the exact night she became pregnant," he said. "I had recently returned from a diplomatic mission encompassing several countries. It was the first time she had allowed me in her bed for several months, and that was only after I pursued the matter of producing an heir."

The tangled web of deceit had now grown, wrapping Maysa in its clutches. If he had been traveling during the time of Rima's actual conception, that left only one probability—Rafiq had not fathered the child she'd been carrying at the time of her demise. "You said something else happened that night. What was it?"

"We debated the announcement for a time," he continued, "and then she informed me she did not care to be pregnant with my child, but she did want out of the marriage. I told her that was impossible and I would not divorce her."

Having heard that from her own husband, Maysa experienced a fleeting moment of sympathy for Rima. "I'm sure that upset her further."

He released a rough sigh. "Yes, but not as much as when I told her if she left the country after the birth, I would seek her out and bring the baby back to the palace. I would see to it she would have no contact with our child. She said she would see me in hell before she allowed that to happen. That is when I ordered her out of the palace. I arranged for the car she was driving that night."

And Maysa knew exactly where she had gone— ironically the resort where they were now having this disturbing discussion. "No one knows about this?"

"Only my assistant, Mr. Deeb, who had the car delivered to the palace." He turned his weary gaze on her. "And now you know everything."

She did, but he did not. She could fill in the blanks, and possibly annihilate everything she had worked so hard to gain, because of one man who had played in integral part in this twisted triangle. Her own flesh and blood.

Rafiq streaked a hand over his jaw and sighed. "I

would not blame you if you choose to leave now and never look back."

She rested a hand on his arm. "If you are expecting harsh judgment from me, you won't find it. You're human and not infallible. Neither am I. We all make mistakes, and we can only move on and learn from those mistakes if they cannot be rectified."

He appeared stunned by the comment. "I deserve no less than your condemnation. What honorable man threatens to tear a mother away from her child, then arranges to send that distraught woman to her death?"

"An angry man," she said. "And you had no way of knowing Rima would have an accident. Her death wasn't your fault any more than your mother's death was your father's fault."

He sighed. "I cannot believe you would forgive me so easily."

"Yet I do, Rafiq. More important, it is past time for you to forgive yourself."

The time had also come to tell him the truth about Rima's relationship with Shamil, and the result of that relationship. But after she consulted the clock on the wall, she decided to wait until she wasn't facing a clinic full of patients in less than twenty minutes. As it stood now, she would probably arrive late.

She came to her feet, leaned over and kissed his cheek. "When I return here tonight, we'll continue this discussion, provided you decide not to end your sabbatical immediately." She held her breath while waiting for his answer.

"I will be here," he said. "I cannot stand the thought of leaving you today."

She couldn't stand the thought of him leaving her

ever. But he might not be so willing to stay once she revealed the truth, as well as how long she had kept it from him. "I have to go now, and I'll see you this evening."

Rafiq rose from the sofa, took her hand and walked her to the door where he kissed her soundly and said goodbye. She hoped it wasn't the final one.

After she was well on her way to the clinic, Maysa mulled over everything Rafiq had told her, particularly the part about Rima lying about the length of her pregnancy. She was without a doubt certain of one thing—Rafiq had not been the father of Rima's child. Her instincts told her she knew the responsible party. And as soon as she had a break at work, she planned to track him down and confront him by phone.

When her cell began to ring, Maysa fished it from her bag to find her brother's name on the screen, as if she had somehow willed him to contact her. "Hello, Shamil," she answered with feigned composure.

"Hello, my dear sister. Are you enjoying your status as the king's whore?"

Evidently the rumors had traveled all the way to Yemen. "It's not like you to listen to idle gossip, Shamil."

"True, but I do tend to believe what I have seen with my own eyes. That was quite a passionate kiss the two of you shared at the door of my finest villa only minutes ago."

Utter panic settled over Maysa. "Where are you now?"

"I am staring at two armored cars, but I am about to pay His Excellency a long overdue visit. I have done some soul-searching during my time away and I have decided the bastard should hear the truth."

Unable to concentrate on driving, Maysa pulled onto the shoulder. "The guards will never let you near him."

"That is where you are wrong. I have already notified the king I will be there soon, and he was more than happy to welcome an old friend."

She highly doubted that. "You call yourself a friend when you have betrayed his trust by sleeping with his wife?"

"You are not one to judge after you have spread your legs for him in *my* resort. I will derive great pleasure from demanding he leave at once."

A sense of dread prompted Maysa to tighten her grasp on the steering wheel. "Shamil, please, think about what you are about to do."

"I have thought about it, and nothing you can say will stop me from exacting the revenge the *king* so deserves."

When the line went dead, Maysa jumped into action. She executed a U-turn in the middle of the road and depressed the accelerator, spewing gravel in her wake. If Shamil made good on this threats, she refused to allow Rafiq to face the truth alone—provided she wasn't already too late.

At one time, Rafiq would have welcomed seeing his onetime closest friend. But after learning from Zain that Shamil was still attempting to thwart the conservation project, he was anything but pleased over his unexpected appearance. "I believe our meeting was scheduled at 4:00 p.m. at the palace."

"And I believe this meeting cannot wait."

When Shamil entered the villa without a proper invitation, both guards immediately moved forward to follow him. Rafiq raised a hand to halt their progress. "Remain here. I will notify you if you are needed."

He returned inside to discover Shamil had made himself at home in a chair across from the divan. "Please, sit down on *my* sofa, Rafiq."

Rafiq complied and assumed a relaxed position, though he was anything but relaxed at the moment. "Your insistence upon calling me by my given name is an act of subordination. I will forgive you this time in light of our shared past."

He stroked his graying beard as if it were a cherished pet. "I am sorry to say I cannot forgive you for seducing my sister. But then I suppose she was an easy target."

The true reason behind the visit had become all too clear. "I refuse to discuss Maysa with you."

Shamil crossed his legs and folded his hands together in his lap. "Perhaps then we should discuss the other woman formerly in your life, until you drove her to an untimely death."

Rafiq clung to the last thread of restraint. "I will not speak to you about Rima, either."

"Then I will speak to you about her. I know everything about your sham of a marriage, Rafiq. Every last detail. Who do you think she told about her misery over being wed to the likes of you?"

He momentarily rejected that notion, until he recalled Rima mentioning having lunch with Shamil a few weeks before her death. "I am aware you and Rima maintained your friendship and that you spoke to her on more than one occasion. We were all friends at one time."

"Friends?" Shamil barked out a caustic laugh. "You were never Rima's friend. You were her captor and she, your prisoner."

Rafiq had begun to suspect Shamil knew much more than he had initially believed. "We were bound by a contract made a long time ago. Rima accepted her role as queen and my wife."

Shamil leaned forward and sneered. "Let me ask you something. Did it disturb you to learn you were not Rima's first lover?"

A repeat of the conversation he had had with Adan a few days before. "What Rima did before our wedding was immaterial to me. I only asked that she remain faithful after we exchanged vows."

"Were you faithful?"

"I was." Though he had been tempted a time or two during the year following their marriage. Yet he had never acted on that temptation.

"Perhaps physically true to her," Shamil said. "But not mentally. You have always lusted after my sister."

"You know not of what you speak." A false denial, but Shamil did not deserve the truth.

"When you were forcing Rima to do your bidding in bed to produce another arrogant Mehdi, were you not imagining driving your *sambool* into Maysa?"

It took all Rafiq's strength not to wrap his hands around Shamil's throat. He settled for a curse. *"Ibn il sharmuta!"*

Shamil appeared only mildly insulted. "Please leave my mother out of this. She was a good woman. Unfortunately, Maysa does not appear to have inherited that goodness. She has brought nothing but shame to our family, first by divorcing her husband, and now by allowing you to bed her."

He refused to acknowledge any intimacy between him and Maysa. He would definitely address Maysa's ruthless ex-husband. "Do you know what Boutros Kassab did to her? Are you aware of the torture he inflicted upon her? Or do you have so little regard for Maysa that you do not care?"

Shamil did not seem the least bit disturbed, leading Rafiq to believe the latter held true. "Maysa has always been prone to exaggeration. I am certain the accusations she leveled against Boutros were overblown."

Having his conjecture confirmed, Rafiq's hatred burned bright for this man whom he once considered a confidant. "At one time I greatly respected you, Shamil. Now I see that you are nothing more than a power-hungry, misguided man without a conscience. It is no wonder you have not found a suitable wife. No woman would dare tie themselves to you."

His smile was cynical. "Your wife did not feel that way, Rafiq. Had she not been bound to your contract, she would have been with me. In fact, she was. Many times when you left her alone to travel. Did you not wonder why she always chose to stay behind?"

He had never questioned her reluctance to travel, nor had he objected to the decision. "She had duties to oversee at the palace."

"She had an aversion to spending time with you. And for your information, I was Rima's first lover, and I was her last."

"You are a liar."

"It is not a lie. She came to me that fateful night

when you ordered her out of the palace. She told me you arranged for her transportation and threatened to take your child away from her."

Rafiq now realized he spoke the truth. "That proves nothing other than she came to you seeking advice."

"She came to me seeking comfort, which I gladly gave to her in my bed. If you require further confirmation, ask my sister."

He had erroneously believed the shocking secrets were over. "What does Maysa have to do with this?"

"She saw Rima and I together in this very place that night."

If Shamil spoke the truth, Rafiq did not understand why Maysa had withheld the information. He intended to find out, but first he must deal with the turncoat before him. "I could have you hanged for this."

Shamil appeared unmoved by the threat. "Yet you will not do that. I hold the power to halt the conservation project, as well as destroy your standing with your people. Once they learn you demanded the queen leave her rightful home, subsequently leading to her death, they will not be quick to forgive you."

Rafiq inherently knew that to be true, but he would not give Shamil the satisfaction of an admission. He would present a defense for his actions. "The people are aware Rima's death was an accident, and I do not need your vote to see the project to fruition since I have the majority of council's support."

"Then consider this. Should word leak out that you have taken a scorned woman as your mistress, then you will take Maysa down with you. Since the day you appointed me health minister, I began to make many contacts in the medical field. I will make certain she is stripped of her hospital privileges and quite possibly her license to practice."

Rafiq glared at him. "You would have to show cause to do that. An unfounded rumor of an affair is not cause."

"Ah, yes, but it is amazing how a proof of physician's grave mistakes can suddenly surface, whether they are founded or not."

His patience now in tatters, Rafiq shot from the sofa and pointed at the door. "Get out."

Shamil's ensuing laugh sounded sinister. "You are ordering me out of my own establishment?"

"Yes, and if you do not leave, I will have you forcefully removed by my guards and have you escorted to the airport. They are very loyal to me, and I have no control over what they might do on the way. A man would have a difficult time surviving in the mountains without supplies, clothes and transportation."

He saw the first sign of fear in Shamil's eyes. "You would not dare give that order, as you would be the primary suspect."

No, he would not, yet he would allow Shamil to believe otherwise. "It is amazing how people mysteriously disappear. Since in all likelihood no one has been made privy to our meeting, and since it is well-known you are currently living in Yemen, you would not be missed for quite some time."

Shamil finally stood, strode to the door and opened it. But before he exited, he faced Rafiq again. "When you see Maysa, give my whore of a sister my fondest regards."

On the heels of his fury, and driven by absolute betrayal, King Rafiq Mehdi, who had always prided himself on control, strode across the room, drew back his fist—and centered it in the middle of Shamil Barad's face.

Nine

Maysa arrived in time to see Rafiq deliver the blow that sent her brother back against one stone column bracing the portico. She watched in horror when the guards restrained Rafiq as he went after Shamil, who used that window of opportunity to throw a punch. The impact to his jaw snapped Rafiq's head back and split the corner of his mouth. Two more sentries appeared from across the road, grabbed Shamil and wrenched his arms behind his back.

Shock kept Maysa momentarily planted in place, until she came around and found the wherewithal to retrieve her medical bag from the backseat. She rushed toward Rafiq, only to be restrained by the bodyguard who had kept Rafiq from mostly doing serious damage to Shamil.

"Unhand her!" Rafiq shouted and then swiped his

shirtsleeve across the trickle of blood seeping from the laceration.

"Did he break my nose, Maysa?" Shamil asked, stopping her progress.

She took a quick glance at the wound. "Yes, it looks broken. They'll take care of it at the emergency room."

"You will not treat it?"

"No, I will not."

"Sharmuta!"

"Perhaps I am a bitch, but at least I fight fairly."

"Take him to the hospital," Rafiq ordered the guards.

For some reason Shamil looked terrified. "I will drive myself."

"You will remain in custody until I decide what I will do in regard to your assault on the king."

"And you will make certain I arrive at the hospital safely?"

Maysa could not believe he was being such a sniveling child. "I will call ahead and inform them you're coming." That would be the only favor she would grant him.

As the security detail began tugging him toward one of the cars, Shamil turned a hateful glare on Rafiq. "Remember what we have discussed, Your Majesty."

Rafiq muttered an Arabic oath as he turned and strode back into the villa before Maysa could get to him. She followed him even knowing she could very well be walking into a hornet's nest, with the king serving as the head hornet.

After she closed the door behind her, Maysa came upon Rafiq restlessly circling the living area, his hands balled into fists as if he would like to hit something else. "Look, Rafiq," she began, "I know you're most likely angry with me—"

"I am not angry with you," he said without looking at her. "I am angry at myself for not maintaining control. For being such a fool and a failure."

"Who have you failed?" she asked, though she already knew the answer.

He finally looked at her, the weight of the kingdom in his eyes. "My wife, and now you."

She set her bag aside on the coffee table, hoping to eventually put it to good use when she treated Rafiq's cut. If he let her treat it. "You and Rima failed each other, Rafiq. You two should never have married in the first place. But you did marry her, she turned to another man, and it all ended in tragedy. No matter what happened that night, it's done and it cannot be undone."

He paused his pacing in the middle of the room. "How long have you known about her affair with Shamil?"

The query came as no surprise. "Not until he told me the day you arrived at my house. I had my suspicions, but I never confirmed them."

"Yet you chose not to tell me."

"Shamil threatened to ruin my medical practice. At the time, that mattered most to me." Before Rafiq had come to matter more. "You and I were barely on speaking terms. I had no idea we would reconnect the way we have."

"Yet when we did become close, you still did not reveal what you knew. You should have said something, Maysa."

"Then you are angry with me."

"Disappointed that you did not feel you could tell

me after what I told you earlier." He both looked and sounded resigned.

"I did plan to tell you tonight, if that's any consolation." And now she was charged with delivering the final betrayal blow. "There is something else you need to know."

"Nothing you could say would surprise me at this point in time."

"Perhaps you should sit down, just in case."

He remained planted in the same spot. "I would rather stand."

Of course he would. "It's about the baby Rima was carrying. Shamil was the father." She waited a moment for the news to sink in before she continued. "I only discovered that this morning, after you mentioned the timing of the pregnancy. Rima was close to entering her second trimester."

"How do you know this?"

Maysa decided she needed to sit and selected the straight-back rattan chair in the corner. "Rima came to me to confirm the pregnancy, although I wasn't certain why. I now believe she wanted to avoid using one of the palace's physicians for fear they would be suspicious since you had been traveling at the time she conceived."

He sighed. "I find little comfort in the knowledge the child was not mine. An innocent life was still taken, regardless of its parentage, and I find that incredibly sad."

The declaration demonstrated the depth of his honor. Some men would be relieved, and not at all upset. "Did Shamil mention the baby to you?"

"He did not, yet I find it hard to believe that Rima would conceal it from him."

Maysa had no problem believing it. "I hate to speak ill of the dead, but Rima was always about appearances. I honestly believe she would not have divorced you for Shamil. She would never put herself in the midst of a scandal. I do think she let him believe she would for the attention."

"The attention I did not give her?"

"It wouldn't have mattered if you'd showered her with it every moment of every day. For Rima, it would never be enough."

"I did not realize you thought so little of her."

Clearly he had been blind to the ongoing competition for his affections between her and Rima. "She craved that attention when we were schoolmates at the palace, and she would find it through whatever means." Including shamelessly flirting with the other two Mehdi brothers behind Rafiq's back. But he had heard enough secrets for one day.

When Maysa noticed Rafiq's lip had begun to swell, she stood and gestured toward the sofa. "I need to take a closer look at your cut."

He trudged toward the divan as if on his way to the gallows. After he settled onto the cushions, Maysa went to work. He winced when she applied antiseptic, yet he remained still when she applied the strips to close the wound.

"That should hold the edges together if you're careful. But if it opens, you may need stitches."

As she began to put away the supplies, Rafiq clasped her wrist. "What are we going to do about us?"

"Is there an us, Rafiq?"

He released her and forked his hands through his hair. "Shamil continues to threaten to expose our affair. We would have to be cautious if we continue to see each other."

If they continued to see each other. "Then I suppose it's probably best we end it now, as originally planned."

"You are willing to walk away after what we have shared?"

She summoned all her courage before she answered. "Yes, because you are not willing to defy tradition and have an open relationship with me."

"To do that would only subject you to constant contempt and ridicule."

"Are you certain you are not referring to yourself?"

"I am the king and will remain so, whatever anyone might believe about me. But I would face resistance from the council when attempting to make decisions for the country. The majority still adhere to the old ways."

"Then in part this is also about your reputation and your unwillingness to discard the old ways."

"I am only trying to protect you, Maysa."

A spear of anger mixed with resentment hurled through her. "I divorced a husband who was basically a terrorist. I left my homeland for a strange country with only the clothes on my back. I worked my way through medical school and returned to Bajul to face the worst possible scorn, and I have survived it all. What makes you believe I need your protection?"

"I care about you and your well-being."

"If you truly cared about me, Rafiq, you would never propose I be your *sharmuta,* as Shamil so aptly put it. That being said, you may consider your sabbatical officially ended, and our affair permanently over. Feel free to return to the palace knowing your secrets are safe with me. Now I have to return to the clinic and salvage what is left of the day." And what was left of her heart.

Fearing she might reconsider or cry, Maysa snatched the bag and headed for the door. She didn't have time to open it before Rafiq came up behind her and slid his arms around her waist. "I do not know how to let you go a second time."

"Then don't, but only on my terms."

He turned her to face him. "I cannot risk failing you the way I failed Rima. I cannot abide you hating me. If avoiding that possibility means letting you go, then I have no choice."

Little by little, her heart began to splinter, one fissure at a time. One word at a time. "Everyone has choices, Rafiq. You have to decide whether you want to risk making them, or if you wish to settle for safety. I will not play second chair in your royal orchestra. I will not stand by while you choose another queen and enter another loveless marriage for the sake of building a fortune and making Mehdi babies. Either we are truly together, or we are not. I need all, or nothing."

She held her breath while she waited to hear his choice, and silently prayed it would be the right one.

Her hopes soared when he held her closely. They plummeted when he said, "I cannot risk hurting you again."

Oh, but he already had. Twice. She pulled away to gain some distance, at least physically. The emotional ties would be much harder to sever. "Then I wish you well, Rafiq, in your endeavors. And please do not try to contact me for I will not accept your calls."

"Will you honor one last request before you leave?"

The pain in his eyes called to her, and she tried not to listen. "That would depend on the request."

"Will you kiss me goodbye?"

Her mind rejected the appeal, while her shattering heart told her to answer. And she would for the sake of what they had meant to each other. A lasting memory to live on until she was ready to move forward.

Maysa wrapped her hand around his neck and brought his lips to hers. They remained that way for a long moment until the threat of tears forced her away from him. "God speed, Rafiq."

"Ana bahebik, habibti."

How long had she waited to hear those words? And now they had come too late. "I love you, too, Rafiq. I have since the first time I saw you. But I find it tragic that we still live in a place where love is simply not enough."

She walked away with her head held high and her soul in tatters. This time, the goodbye hadn't broken her. Not completely.

In the two weeks since Maysa had told Rafiq goodbye, she'd immersed herself in work, thankful for the diversion. Yet the nights had been the most difficult, and uninterrupted sleep had been at a premium.

Fortunately, today she finally felt more like her old self and prepared to meet any challenges. She was not prepared for the patient seated on the exam room table. "What are you doing here, Madison?"

"Guess."

Maysa didn't dare. "I hope you have a cold or some other minor ailment."

Madison tightened the band securing her blond

ponytail. "I'm not sure what I have exactly. I've been a little queasy in the morning and tired. But then being a mother to triplets can be exhausting."

Apparently the overtired mother was having a mental lapse. "You mean twins."

"I'm counting the father of my babies, so that basically makes three children. Did you know the man has no clue how to fold towels?"

She smiled. "Of course not. Someone has always done it for him."

"That someone is me because I refuse to have the staff do something I am quite capable of doing."

As much as she wanted to visit with Zain's wife, she still had six more patients to see before day's end. "Back to your symptoms. Is it possible you could be pregnant?"

"I have no idea. My periods are still irregular even after my one functioning ovary spit out double deuces."

"Let me rephrase the question then. Have you had unprotected sexual intercourse?"

Madison looked more than a bit sheepish. "Yes. The day we went to the lake."

The day they had stopped by to reveal the rumor mill was in full spin. "I knew I should have given you condoms."

"Zain hates using condoms."

"So does Raf..." She wanted to yank her wayward tongue out of her mouth. "Many men take exception to them, but they're necessary if you wish to prevent disease and pregnancy."

"It's okay," Madison said. "I know you and Rafiq were sleeping together. I could tell the minute I saw the two of you together at your house."

"Actually, we weren't sleeping together at that time."

"But you did sleep together later, right?"

Maysa grasped for an excuse to change the subject. "Let's get you a pregnancy test, just in case." She turned to the counter, retrieved the box, then offered it to Madison. "You know the drill. The restroom is right across the hall."

"Gotta love peeing on a stick," she said as she hopped off the table and headed out the door.

While Madison was gone, Maysa debated whether she should ask about Rafiq. Probably unwise. She would hate to learn he had already begun the queen candidate search.

After Madison returned, Maysa placed the test on the counter and set the portable timer to await the results. "In ten minutes, we should have the answer."

Madison scooted back onto the table and sent her dangling legs into motion. "I'm having a moment of déjà vu from the last time you gave me a pregnancy test. We have to stop meeting like this."

Maysa laughed. "I agree, but it's better than if you had something serious, such as malaria."

"Very true."

A few moments of awkward silence ticked off before Maysa spoke again. "How are the children?"

"Fine. Getting fat as little pigs."

"And Zain is doing well? Other than his domestic issues."

"Very well and frisky as ever. He has been busy with the water project, but he's never too tired for... you know."

Yes, she definitely knew, and she couldn't quell the envy onset. She studied the anatomy poster on the wall to her left in an effort to avoid Madison's scrutiny. "Elena and Adan are doing well?"

"Yes, and it's okay if you ask about him, Maysa."

Could she possibly be more obvious? "All right. How is he?"

Madison scowled. "He's horrible. He has turned into the meanest king in all the Middle East. He orders everyone around nonstop and refuses to come to dinner. And that blasted pacing. Makes me want to glue his butt to the office chair."

She smiled in part over Madison's comment, and in part because she liked to think Rafiq was experiencing some regret over his decision. "The pacing is a longtime habit. He's nervous."

"He's lovesick. He misses you, Maysa. I don't really know what happened between you, and you certainly are under no obligation to tell me."

She needed to tell someone, and she felt she could trust Zain's wife with the information. "Archaic tradition happened. He can't be openly involved with a divorcée, and I refuse to be his mistress."

"I don't blame you." Madison suddenly shifted her weight from one hip to the other, a possible sign of discomfort. "I do know about Rima and your brother's ongoing affair, and that the baby wasn't Rafiq's."

"Rafiq told you that?" she asked, attempting to temper the shock in her voice.

Madison shook her head. "No. He told Zain, and Zain told me. We don't have any secrets between us. He's also concerned that if Shamil decides to leak the information, I'll have to do damage control."

"It could definitely be damaging, depending on how

the information is perceived. The country seemed to take a liking to Rima immediately."

"I personally never cared for her," Madison said. "She seemed a bit self-absorbed at times, and cold. But then maybe I'm being too harsh. I never really had the chance to know her that well."

Maysa had known her all too well. "She's always been aloof since our teenage years."

"Then you knew her before she and Rafiq became engaged? Or maybe I should say before they went under contract."

"Actually, Rafiq and I were seeing each other up to that point in time." And after, a fact she decided not to divulge. "We were very close."

Madison sent her a sympathetic look. "It must have been difficult knowing she was taking your man right out from under you, and you could do nothing about it."

"It was very difficult, and at times it seemed she went out of her way to flirt with Rafiq in my presence. But then we were teenage girls, and you know how petty they can be sometimes."

"Speaking of teenagers, did you know Rima slept with Adan when he was only seventeen?"

She could tell Madison regretted the statement the moment it left her mouth. And Maysa had a difficult time believing Adan would betray his own brother.

"Are you certain that really happened?"

"Positive. Adan told me the night of the wedding. He claims Rima had argued with her one true love and she turned to him for comfort. Adan being Adan, he jumped at the opportunity. When I mistakenly thought he meant she'd argued with Rafiq, he hinted someone else was involved. I assume that someone else was your brother."

That made perfect sense to Maysa. "Does Rafiq know?"

"Not hardly, and I hope Adan doesn't have a sudden crisis of conscience and blurt it out. That would probably send Rafiq right over the edge. Losing you has been bad enough. That's why I wish you could work it out and save us all some grief."

She saw no end to the impasse. "In order to work it out, one of us will have to give in, and it will not be me. I highly doubt Rafiq will, either."

"You never know, Maysa. Just look at what Zain did to be with me. He gave up the crown and moved back to America."

Rafiq would never do something so drastic when it involved duty. That much she knew.

When the timer dinged, Maysa walked to the counter and picked up the test to read it. "This is either good news, or not so good news. You'll have to tell me which one it might be."

The woman looked as though she might vault off the exam table. "I'll let you know as soon as you tell me what it says."

"You're not pregnant."

Madison's shoulders slumped. "In a way, I'm a little disappointed. In a bigger way, I'm glad. I'm not sure either Zain or I could handle having another baby after dealing with twins. At least not for another year or two."

Maysa tossed the test into the trash and smiled. "If that happens, you must be sure to confirm the pregnancy with me. We'll make it our own tradition."

"And maybe before then, you'll be the one in need of a pregnancy test."

Not likely. "Single mothers are not always viewed favorably, and I don't intend to look for a husband in the near future."

"You could always go the artificial insemination route." Madison snapped her fingers and pointed. "You could even do it yourself."

That appealed to Maysa about as much as having a tooth filled. "No, thank you. I'm also fairly sure sperm donors are few and far between in Bajul."

"I know of one man who would gladly donate his sperm the natural way. Of course, he'll first have to realize he's in danger of giving up the best thing that has ever happened to him, meaning you."

"Forgive me if I don't hold my breath until that happens. I'd require a ventilator."

Madison slid off the table, gave her a hug and paused before she left the room. "Don't give up on him yet, Maysa. He just might come around, marry you and tell all of Bajul to go to hell if they don't like it."

As far as Maysa was concerned, that would take a full-fledged miracle. And though she had witnessed a few miracles in her career—the birth of a child, a patient's unexpected recovery from a devastating illness—she wouldn't let allow herself to hope for one this time.

Ten

"Miracle of all miracles. You are actually sitting down."

At the sound of the grating British accent, Rafiq looked up from his notes to see Adan filing into the office, Zain and Madison trailing behind him. "I do not recall summoning any of you."

Zain claimed the chair across from the desk without seeking Rafiq's permission. "Since you did not summon us in response to our request for a family meeting, we have taken the initiative to seek you out."

Rafiq gripped the gold pen in both hands with enough force to break it in half. "The council meeting will be held tomorrow afternoon, and I need to prepare. Therefore, this meeting is officially over."

Adan assumed his usual perch on the edge of the desk, as if he had been raised by baboons. "We are not leaving until we have our say, Rafiq."

If he chose to argue the point, he would only prolong their departure. "Then have your say and be done with it. But make it quick or I will leave the whole lot of you here, retire to my bedroom and lock the door."

While Madison remained a few feet away, Zain and Adan exchanged a glance before Zain began to speak. "We are here on Maysa's behalf."

The sound of her name instantly filled Rafiq with further regret. The same regret that had haunted him every moment of every day since they had parted. "She has contacted you?"

"She has no idea we're discussing her," Adan said. "However, since you apparently have left her high and dry, we feel it is necessary to advocate for her. In other words, remove your head from that part of your anatomy in which no self-respecting head belongs, and beg her to come back to you."

If only that option existed. "Impossible. Any public connection she has with me will only serve to destroy her good standing in the community. She has already endured entirely too much hardship as it is." Some of which he had recently imposed on her life.

"If you're referring to her status as a divorcée," Zain began, "it's a common occurrence in America. People change spouses as often as they change underwear."

His brother had clearly forgotten he was in Bajul, not Los Angeles. "Need I remind you we are not governed by the same laws and customs here?"

"No, you need not," Zain said. "I personally experienced the results of those antiquated customs. Perhaps I should remind you that I chose to marry Madison, and we have suffered no serious ill effects from that decision."

"You are no longer king, Zain. You handed that honor to me. My private life is put under a microscope daily, and I will not subject Maysa to constant scrutiny."

"Instead, you are willing to subject all of us to your bad temper because you are so consumed with her, you can barely function," Zain said.

His ever-present anger began to escalate. "My duty has not been affected by my decision to cut all ties with her." The decision that she truthfully had made for him.

Adan scowled. "Duty be damned, Rafiq. Your duty cannot replace a woman's affections, or save you from your determination to punish the world for your own failures."

He did not need to be reminded how he had failed, or whom he had failed. "If you know what is good for you, Adan, you will go fly a plane and leave me be."

Madison raised her hand as if they were in a schoolroom, not the king's official office. "May I say something, Rafiq?"

He waved her forward. "Please. Everyone should have the opportunity to take a verbal shot at the king."

"That's not my intent," she said. "I simply wanted to let you know that when I've taken the twins for a stroll in the village, I've managed to talk with several of your subjects. They all seem to feel you are doing an excellent job."

"I am pleased to hear that." The first good news he had heard in quite some time, aside from Maysa's declaration of love. "All the more reason not to introduce a scandal."

Madison's gaze momentarily faltered. "I also took the liberty of digging into Boutros Kassab's history.

According to a few contacts I have in Europe, it seems he has a history of violence against women, specifically two of his three ex-wives and one mistress. Of course, he used his influence to get the charges dismissed."

"He is a known tyrant, so I am not surprised." He *was* surprised that Madison knew about Maysa's marriage to Boutros. Perhaps too much to be the product of a natural curiosity.

His suspicions were confirmed when she glanced at her husband before bringing her attention back to Rafiq. "Since Maysa suffered abuse at the hands of Kassab, we could leak that information. Then when you decide to publicly announce your relationship, people would know the reason behind Maysa's divorce."

He had been wrong to confide in Zain. "You told her about what Maysa endured when I emphatically asked that you not share that information?"

Zain seemed unmoved by Rafiq's ire. "Madison and I have no secrets. She is only attempting to aid in your happiness, and you will never be happy until you are reunited with Maysa."

When Zain stood and wrapped a protective arm around her shoulder, Madison said, "Thank you, sweetheart. And by the way, Maysa confirmed we're not pregnant."

Zain kissed her on the mouth, as if no one else mattered. The same way Rafiq had kissed Maysa only two short weeks ago.

"Then we shall have more time to practice in the next year or two," Zain said after they parted.

"Good lord," Adan said. "If you two do not stop this nonsense, I will send you both to your room and sell your children to the highest bidder."

Zain shot an acrid glance at Adan. "You are jealous because you have not kept company with a female in quite some time. Perhaps you should take care of that and leave the adults to solve Rafiq's problems."

As the brotherly bickering continued, Rafiq's temper arrived in the form of a solid slam on the desk. "Enough! I am capable of solving my own problems, and I am tired of the intrusion." He regarded Zain's wife. "Madison, I appreciate your assistance, but I will not be in need of the information. Revealing Kassab's tainted history will only force Maysa to relive a past she desires to forget and open old wounds that have finally begun to heal." Until he had inflicted the emotional wounds upon her.

"I understand your decision," Madison said. "And you can trust me to keep the information confidential."

Rafiq came to his feet and willed his anger to calm. "I am finished answering questions and entertaining suggestions, so if you will excuse me—"

"Not until you answer my questions, *cara mia.*"

As always, his former governess had an uncanny knack of appearing before Rafiq could escape the inquest. "I will allow one more question from you, Elena. But only one."

She wedged between a surprised Madison and Zain. "You will answer as many questions as I ask. First, do you love Maysa?"

He tracked his gaze from one expectant face to the other. "With all due respect, that is a private matter I will not address."

"Bloody hell, Rafiq," Adan said. "Just admit it."

"I assure you the sky will not fall on your head if

you say the words," Zain added. "Otherwise, I would have suffered several concussions."

"Do you love her?" Elena repeated.

"Yes, I love her." With all his once-hardened heart. "Are you satisfied now?"

The woman looked extremely satisfied, and somewhat smug. "Do you love her enough to spit in the face of convention and claim her as your partner for all time?"

When he failed to answer, Elena marched forward and stood immediately before the desk. "Rafiq, you have two choices, the first being you can disregard public opinion and ask Maysa to marry you because I know *she* is strong enough to handle any repercussions. Are you?"

He did not view that as a viable option. "And my second choice?"

"You can end up like me. Alone."

"You have never seemed to have an issue with being alone before."

"I was never truly physically alone, Rafiq, but I was lonely. I spent a lifetime loving a man who refused to acknowledge our affair for fear of upsetting the royal applecart."

His mind was fraught with more confusion. "What man is this, Elena?"

"Our father, you fool," Adan said. "I have suspected as much for years."

Elena looked completely baffled. "How could you have known?"

"I arrived late from the academy one night and I saw you enter his suite," Adan stated matter-of-factly.

"I assumed everyone knew and just never mentioned it out of respect for your privacy."

"Then you were the one sleeping with the king?" Zain asked, his tone heralding the shock Rafiq now experienced.

Elena lifted her chin, her eyes slightly misted with tears. "Yes, I was sleeping with the king. Right up until the day before he died. And no, I was not responsible for his death. I *was* responsible for giving him many memorable moments during his final hours on earth."

Adan kissed her cheek. "Good show, old girl. And while we're confessing…" He turned to address Rafiq. "I wish to apologize for sleeping with your wife."

The shock returned with the force of a grenade. "You did what?"

Adan held up his hands, palms forward. "Before you come across the desk to slug me, I wish to add I was only seventeen at the time. Rima apparently had a tussle with Shamil and she looked to me for comfort. I did not plan it, and neither did she."

If he heard one more revelation, he would not be responsible for what he would do to his youngest sibling. "You also knew Rima and Shamil were lovers?"

He shrugged. "I assumed everyone knew—"

"You assume too much, Adan," Zain said.

Adan presented a wry smile. "Obviously."

Rafiq turned a glare and a question on Zain. "Do you wish to confess anything?"

Zain held up his hands in surrender. "I solemnly swear I did not bed your former wife."

"I am so glad to know that, honey," Madison said.

So was Rafiq, if he could actually believe Zain. He no longer knew what to believe.

"It is now time to put the past to rest." Elena braced her palms on the desk, leaned forward and directed her gaze at Rafiq. "*Cara,* you have shown signs of being a great leader, yet most likely not greater than your father. But you can be a better man than your father. You can have the life you were meant to lead with Maysa, or you can enter into another loveless marriage and be miserable until your time on earth is over."

Or he could spend the rest of his life alone. He had no need to produce an heir, now that Zain had fulfilled that requirement. His father had completed his reign as a widower, and no one had condemned him for the decision. Of course, no one had known about his relationship with Elena. Yet he had dishonored the cherished surrogate mother to Rafiq and his brothers by not standing up to the elders and making a commoner his queen.

"I will consider all that you have said," he told Elena, the only answer he could presently give.

Elena straightened and smoothed a hand over her graying hair. "That is all anyone can ask. And I know you will make the right decision for all concerned, as I have taught you to do. Never forget what makes a man a true king and a hero. Honor."

And he had clearly forgotten that honor over the past few weeks. "If it is all the same to you, I wish to be alone now."

"Let us leave your brother to his thoughts," Elena said as she started toward the door, gesturing for everyone to follow her.

And everyone did, except for Zain. "I do have to know one more thing, Rafiq."

He released a weary sigh. "I am in no mood to answer more questions about Maysa."

"This doesn't involve Maysa," he said. "It does involve her brother. Why have you not yet dismissed him from the council?"

If he did, he risked Shamil revealing damning information to the press about his relationship with Maysa. Yet if he decided to make it known to the world that he was in love with the beautiful doctor, and he planned to make her the next queen, that would no longer be a concern. But the possible uproar over taking that course could be very concerning.

Since he had not quite reached that decision, Rafiq provided only a partial truth. "I had thought to ask him to step down first. If he does not, then I will demand his resignation."

"I personally would opt to humiliate him tomorrow at the meeting by relieving him of his duties," Zain said. "Perhaps he will then think twice before he tangles with another Mehdi and receives another broken nose."

After Zain exited the room, Rafiq weighed his brother's suggestion. He agreed that dismissing Shamil publicly would be effective, and worth considering. First, he had to determine whether he would attempt to reestablish a relationship with Maysa. A permanent, public relationship.

With that consideration rolling around in his mind, Rafiq would be forced to face another sleepless night— without Maysa. Would he be wise to ask her to make it his last?

You have shown signs of being a great leader, yet

most likely not greater than your father.... You can have the life you were meant to lead with Maysa....

Elena's words of wisdom suddenly struck a chord in Rafiq. He could be a better man. Maysa could assist him with that. In some ways, she already had. She was stronger than most men he had known, at times even him. Determined and intelligent. Worthy of respect. She had much to offer this country. She had much more to offer him. Much more than he probably deserved.

Rafiq could not bear the thought of spending another long day—and night—without Maysa Barad. Now that he had made the supreme decision to alter tradition, as well as his life, he had to formulate a plan. As the kernel of an idea filtered into his brain, a scheme that would cover two pressing issues at once, he smiled for the first time in weeks. He prayed that what he had planned would bring about Maysa's smile, too.

She wasn't particularly thrilled to be summoned to the palace by Rafiq's assistant, Mr. Deeb. Yet when Maysa had learned she was expected to speak on current health care issues before the royal council, her attitude immediately changed. She could not wait to enlighten each and every one of them.

And now here she was, waiting in the anteroom for her turn to finally have the chance to give the members a good dose of her reality. Unfortunately, the opportunity meant she would have to face Rafiq, as well as her brother, who amazingly still held his position on the governing board. Despite his verbal threats, and his physical assault on the king, Shamil had somehow come out of the situation smelling like a rose, while she still carried the thorns of Rafiq's rejection.

Maysa refused to worry over that now. She would walk into the room as the only woman among all men and let them know she was a force to be reckoned with. Her bravado began to diminish when Deeb appeared at the main door. "They are ready for you now, Dr. Barad."

And she was ready for them—for the most part.

After silently demanding her nerves be still, Maysa entered displaying a confidence she didn't exactly feel. To make matters worse, Rafiq happened to be the first person to invade her field of vision. And what a vision he was, dressed in his finest black silk suit, the official sash of the king draped around his neck, his face free of facial hair, his dark eyes without obvious emotion. She had no idea what he was feeling, only what she was feeling for him—undeniable longing.

"Gentlemen," he began in Arabic. "You all know Dr. Barad."

Maysa took inventory of their reactions and wasn't pleased with the results. No one spoke a greeting aside from Zain and Adan, although a few nodded in acknowledgment.

Rafiq pulled out the chair next to his and gestured her forward. After she settled in, she realized she was now face-to-frown with her brother. Lovely.

She turned her attention to the king as he outlined future plans for hospital expansion and patiently waited for her turn to present her thoughts on rural health care.

But before that turn arrived, Rafiq centered a bitter gaze on Shamil. "Sheikh Barad, as presiding Minister of Health, it is my opinion you have failed in successfully overseeing Bajul's faltering health care system."

Shamil's face turned so red, Maysa feared his head

might explode. "I take exception to your criticism, Your Excellency. I have served our people well."

"I disagree," Rafiq said, switching to English. "And I take exception to you sleeping with the queen, you traitorous son of a bitch."

Maysa had no way of knowing how many members understood the English curse, but she understood it very well. However, she had never heard Rafiq speak the words before, and she found it somewhat amusing, and appropriate for the situation.

Her brother stood so abruptly, he knocked his chair back in the process. "You are out of line, Rafiq."

Rafiq remained surprisingly calm. "And you are hereby facing charges of high treason if you do not vacate your position, and the premises, immediately."

Shamil sent a pointed look at Maysa before returning his ugly sneer to the king. "You are willing to make my sister your sacrificial lamb?"

A slightly mocking smile curled the corners of Rafiq's mouth. "No, but I am willing to appoint her as the new health minister, if she agrees."

Maysa looked around at all the confused men lining the table. But she didn't know if their confusion resulted from Rafiq offering a woman a position on the council for the first time in Bajul's history, or because Rafiq still spoke in English. "I would be honored, Your Majesty." Honored and thrilled and amazed.

"This is a travesty!" Shamil shouted. "A monumental mistake for this nation!"

"And men like you are a scourge on our nation," Rafiq said as he signaled a nearby guard, then returned to speaking in their native tongue. "Escort the sheikh to the airport and inform them that by my order, he is permanently barred from crossing Bajul's borders."

Shamil shook off the guard's grasp and pointed a shaky finger at Maysa. "You will regret this decision, and you will suffer the wrath of the people once they learn you are the king's secret whore. They will shun you."

"Not if she is the queen."

Shamil looked stunned, while Maysa turned wide eyes on Rafiq. "What did you say?"

"I am unofficially asking you to be my wife." And he did so where everyone could understand his proposal. "I will do the official honors after the meeting. You may give me your answer at that time."

As security escorted a cursing Shamil out of the room, Maysa sat in shocked silence. Yet several members of the council broke theirs by issuing protests over both Rafiq's decisions.

He commanded their attention by rapping the table with his palm. "Silence! I ask who among you has the right to judge Dr. Barad when she has done nothing but divorce a tormentor and care for the poorest of our people. Who among you has given more than your wealth to do the same?"

"She is a harlot who has taken the king as her lover," one man said. "She is a divorced woman who has no respect for the sanctity of marriage."

Rafiq glared at him. "And you do, Sheikh Saab? Do you not dishonor your wife nightly by bedding the innkeeper's wife?" He then turned to another protester. "And you, Sheikh Najem. Did you not divorce your first wife to marry a woman much younger than yourself?"

Najem looked as if he would like to disappear beneath the conference table. "It is different. I am a man."

"And that is where we differ," Rafiq said. "Both my brothers and myself believe we are overdue implementing changes in attitude when it comes to the backbone of this country, women such as Dr. Barad."

Zain and Adan verbally added their support before Rafiq spoke again. "Now that the business at hand is settled, including going forward with the water project, this meeting is officially adjourned."

Before Maysa could mentally digest the chaotic events, Rafiq took her by the hand, led her through the lengthy first-floor corridor, and up the stairs at a fast clip. He slowed a bit as they climbed to the third floor, but not enough for Maysa to catch her breath or gather her thoughts.

She suddenly realized they had arrived at the royal living quarters when she peered through the open bedroom door to her right. "What just happened in that meeting?"

"You agreed to become Bajul's newly appointed health minister to replace your brother, whom I have permanently exiled."

"And?"

He hinted at a smile. "I unofficially asked you to be my wife, and now I wish to make it official." Like a storybook hero, the king of Bajul went to one knee and clasped both her hands in his. "Maysa Barad, will you do me the honor of being my wife and my queen?"

She'd imagined this moment many times in her youth, and "youth" was the key. Now she was an adult, with adult concerns.

"Well?" Rafiq asked with a touch of impatience in his tone.

She wanted to say yes, but she wasn't quite ready to do that. "I'm still thinking."

He stood, his expression showing his disappointment. "I have asked too much of you, and I have waited until it is too late."

"I didn't say no, Rafiq. But before I say yes, I have to know what changed your mind."

"Not what, but whom," he said. "Elena forced me to see the error of my ways, immediately after she revealed she carried on a long-time affair with my father, who refused to make her his wife due to outdated mores."

Maysa was quickly reaching revelation overload. "How did they pull that off without anyone finding out?"

"Adan claims he knew, but Zain and I only heard rumors that our father had a mistress. We never suspected it would be the woman who raised us."

She, too, had heard the rumors, yet never in a million years would she have guessed Elena as the mystery woman. "It's sad to know that she was never able to show her love for your father out in the open."

"And that is what I am trying to avoid with us. I understand that I am asking you to endure continued bias, and I would not blame you if you refused me—"

"Let me stop you right there. As I've said before, I have survived much worse than a few insults. I survived the members' caustic remarks in the meeting only a few minutes ago. But if I agree to marry you, I will continue to be who I am, not who everyone feels

I should be. I will still be a doctor, and I will insist on treating the patients who need me."

Rafiq streak a hand over his jaw. "You realize that will require a security contingency at the clinic at all times."

That was something Maysa had yet to consider. "I accept that necessity, as long as the men do not frighten away my patients."

"They will also be required to accompany us when we travel to the outlying areas."

"We?"

His smile arrived, fully formed and completely gorgeous. "Yes, we. I believe I still have much to learn about our country's medical needs. Who better to guide me than you? However, I will make certain we have better accommodations, or at the very least, a comfortable cot for the tent where I will make love to you the next time."

"I will definitely agree to that, Your Majesty."

His features turned suddenly serious. "Then you will agree to marry me?"

She saw no harm in keeping him in suspense for a while longer. "I am leaning in that direction."

He slipped his arms around her waist and tugged her closer. "Maysa, if you refuse me, and I pray you do not, you must know I will never marry another. I refuse to settle for less than what we have together, an abiding love that has spanned years of separation. I will never feel for another woman the depth of what I feel for you. I simply cannot."

That alone convinced Maysa to deliver a resounding "Yes, I will marry you."

They sealed this unlikely betrothal, not with a contract, but with a kiss, as it should be. That kiss ended when a household staff member cleared her throat before she rushed by.

"Let us retire to my bedroom now," Rafiq said as soon as the woman disappeared around the corner.

Maysa glanced at the open door, specifically the bed, and questioned the wisdom in his plan. "I'm not sure I would be comfortable doing that, Rafiq."

"She never slept in my bed, Maysa," he said, as if he had channeled her concern. "I suppose I have been saving the bed for you, though it took me a while to realize I have been waiting for you all my life."

"And I am honored you reserved the permanent space beside you." As well as deeply touched.

"If you are also worried that I am only interested in making love to you," he added, "and I used a marriage proposal to achieve that goal, I assure you that is not the case. I have simply not been able to sleep without you in my arms."

Such a sweet thing to admit, but Maysa was still a bit suspicious. "It's a little past four o'clock, Rafiq. Isn't it too early to retire for the night?"

He presented an endearing grin, with a side of sexy devil tossed in for good measure. "Perhaps we could consider it a long nap?"

Now that her adrenaline level had plummeted, Maysa could probably nap standing up. She released Rafiq and stretched her arms above her heads. "I am very tired, so I suppose we could manage that."

Rafiq then swept Maysa into his arms, carried her into his bedroom as if she were already his bride and laid her on the bed for their "nap." After they undressed down to only skin, they did actually sleep for a while before they officially made love as an engaged couple. A soft, sensuous lovemaking session that almost brought Maysa to tears. Joyful tears.

And in the peaceful moments that followed, they were content to hold each other as if they had no other plans for the foreseeable future—until Maysa remembered they did have one monumental plan to make.

"When do you suggest we have the wedding, King Mehdi?"

He nuzzled her neck. "Tomorrow would be preferable, unless we can find someone to officiate tonight."

She elbowed Rafiq's side, causing him to release an exaggerated wince. "I am serious."

"And I am now injured, as well as serious about wanting to marry you quickly, before you change your mind. But I suppose we need sufficient time to make the arrangements."

"We only need a month at best," she said. "Just enough time to organize a small, intimate ceremony. Perhaps we should consider traveling south to the beach, or perhaps here at the lake. I have always thought it would be nice to marry without shoes."

Rafiq lifted his head from the pillow and frowned. "You do not wish to wear shoes or have an elaborate undertaking?"

"I wish anything but a large wedding. We have both been through the pomp and circumstance before. I see no need to repeat that now. And yes, I want to marry without my shoes and feel warm sand beneath my feet."

"I will leave the decision to discard footwear to you. But when a Mehdi king takes a new queen, he is expected to hold a large celebration in honor of the event, complete with a feast and thousands of people, most of whom he has never met, nor does he care to meet."

That was not Maysa's idea of a good time. "I will agree to the feast and the hordes of strangers, as long as we exchange our vows in private with only close friends and family in attendance."

He scowled. "I hope family does not include your brother."

"Bite your tongue, future husband. I would rather consume a plateful of salt than have Shamil at our wedding."

He kissed her gently. "I agree, my future queen. Your brother is not welcome in our world."

She smiled. "And for future reference, I prefer to be addressed as Dr. Queen. I believe I have earned the title."

Rafiq laughed then—a rich, deep laugh that provided masculine music to Maysa's ears. "As you wish, Dr. Queen," he said, followed by a lingering kiss. "And I believe I have thought of the perfect setting for our wedding ceremony."

"That cove by the lake?"

"No. The place where we began our journey together. Our past."

Epilogue

Exactly one month later, the reigning king and the physician queen exchanged vows, surrounded by olive trees and fifty or so of their closest friends and family. The bride had exchanged her preferred gauze dresses for a gown made of champagne-colored silk. The groom sported an open-collared, white tailored shirt with a beige jacket and slacks. Neither wore shoes, a sincere scandal in the making.

Maysa's attendants, Madison and Demetria, wore aqua dresses, while Zain and Adan reluctantly donned matching navy suits to meet their responsibility as groomsmen. None of the bridal party appreciated the no-shoe policy, a true uprising in the making.

Perhaps the ceremony wasn't quite as intimate as Maysa would have liked, but everything was going as planned...until two international news helicopters began buzzing overhead, forcing them to hurry their vows and the official kiss.

The disruption sent everyone to their awaiting cars for the brief trip to the palace. A trip too brief for the bride to agree to the groom's suggestion they begin the honeymoon on the journey. Just as well, Maysa decided. Had she agreed, the wedding guests would probably see guilt written all over her face.

Moments later, the newlyweds entered the massive banquet hall to a round of rousing applause. Maysa was extremely thankful for the show of approval and somewhat surprised. Fortunately, the press coverage had been favorable, and she hadn't been exposed to overt hostility, aside from the palace chef, who had not been pleased when she'd changed her mind about the menu twice.

Maysa could not recall being so blissfully happy, or so ready to begin her life with Rafiq. First, she had to assume her first duty as the queen—mingling with some of the most influential people in the world.

She spent well over an hour exchanging polite greetings with guests who'd waited a long while in the lengthy reception line to meet the monarchs. During a brief break in the line's flow, she surveyed the decorations made from bouquets of fragrant jasmine and the candles set out on the tables. And when one esteemed, unfamiliar guest held Rafiq captive with endless chatter, she turned her attention to the bounty of food spread out on the nearby tables. Enough food to feed half of Bajul, and she would swear more than half had come. By the time the last well-wisher left, she was ready to consume her fair share. Unfortunately, Rafiq had been detained again, this time by a woman at least twenty years his senior. That didn't stop her from fawning all over him, and Maysa didn't mind a bit. After this free-for-all food fest ended, the king would be taking her to Cyprus for two weeks filled with sea, sand and on-demand sex.

Thinking about the honeymoon led her to seek out her husband. When he caught her gaze and winked, she considered dragging him away now, a very unqueenly thing to do.

"Have you been enjoying your first hours as the queen?"

Maysa turned to Madison and frowned. "I am not enjoying having to wear these high heels. I'm definitely not enjoying the limited time with my new husband."

"They both take some getting used to," Madison said as she acknowledged a guest with a wave. "Both the heels on your feet, and the human kind who think it's their right to have the king's ear, even when that king is the groom."

Madison waved yet again, this time at a handsome, middle-aged gentleman. "I have no idea who that was," she said through a fake grin. "Some dignitary I invited I think. I believe he's from Albania, or maybe it's Australia. First rule of thumb, smile and pretend you know them, even if you don't."

"That's what I've been doing since we arrived, and I didn't understand what some of them said to me. It's a true disadvantage."

"I'll be glad to teach you some basic foreign greetings if you'd like," Madison said. "I know at least fifty."

"You and Zain will return to California before I master even five."

Madison brought her attention from the crowd and

gave it to Maysa. "Actually, we've decided to stay in Bajul indefinitely."

Maysa decided her sister-in-law deserved a hug for delivering such glad tidings. "I'm thrilled to know you're staying. I'm going to need all the support I can get. Rafiq will be pleased, too. But exactly why did you decide to relocate from Los Angeles and leave the beach behind?"

"We want the children to be raised here so they can learn about their heritage. And I want Cala to lead the future generation of Bajul's kick-ass women, just like her aunt Maysa, who defied all odds and received the ultimate prize."

"Rafiq?"

Madison frowned. "No. Premium tickets to the local sheepherder's ball."

Maysa grinned. "I was not aware of that perk."

"Of course I meant Rafiq, silly queen. He's always been considered quite a catch, just like Zain before he came to his senses and married me." Something, or someone, behind Maysa drew Madison's attention. "Speaking of our catches, here they come, plus the lone bachelor prince who mysteriously went missing after the wedding."

Maysa turned to see the approaching trio of gorgeous Mehdi brothers. Rafiq and Zain's resemblance to each other had always been remarkable, but even more so now that her husband decided not to regrow his goatee. Yet Adan, with his lighter-colored hair and skin tone, as well as his deep, deep dimples, did not favor his siblings aside from his tall stature and distinctive gait. Clearly he had inherited his looks from some unknown relative.

After Rafiq came to Maysa's side and kissed her soundly, Adan inserted himself between them. "Congratulations to the bride," he said, then leaned to kiss Maysa's cheek. "And my apologies for my tardiness in arriving here tonight."

Rafiq demonstrated his disapproval with a scowl and showed his possessive side by wrapping one arm around Maysa's waist and pulling her close to his side. "May I ask where you went after we left the grove?"

Adan adjusted his collar that seemed perfectly fine. "Since I am a gentleman, I will only say that I was preoccupied with a lovely little lady right here in the palace, and she is quite charming."

"Only you could manage to pick up a woman in less than an hour's time," Zain said.

Adan grinned. "Yes, I definitely picked her up."

Zain pointed at him. "Enjoy your freedom now, because mark my words, I predict you will soon meet that special someone and she'll drag you onto the marriage merry-go-round." When Madison glared at him, he added, "I meant she will introduce you to the state of marital bliss."

"You are wrong, brother," Adan said. "I intend to adhere to my plan of waiting until I am at least forty before I settle down. And as of this evening, I have decided to remain celibate for a while."

"That will most likely be the longest ten minutes of your life," Rafiq said, drawing laughter from everyone but Adan. "Now that the festivities seem to be dying down, have you notified the airport of our impending departure?"

"I have and the plane is ready and waiting." Adan began to back away as he spoke. "And I am prepared to deliver you to your destination safe and sound, after I say goodbye to the lady."

"Hurry," Rafiq called after his brother before Adan disappeared through the double doors.

Madison pushed up her sheer sleeve and checked her watch. "The celibacy thing didn't even last seven minutes."

The conversation continued until Adan suddenly returned with a beautiful baby girl wearing a pink satin dress, her thumb planted securely in her mouth. But not just any baby—Zain and Madison's baby girl, Cala.

He walked up to the group, a mischievous look splashed across his face. "Did I not say she was special?"

Zain kissed his daughter's cheek. "The most special lady in the world, and the niece of quite the deceiver."

Madison moved closer to examine Cala's dress. "Where did this come from?"

Adan's grin expanded. "I saw it in a boutique window the last time I visited Paris. I could not resist buying it for her. I bought Joseph a miniature tuxedo for the occasion. He's wearing it now, but unfortunately he passed out in Elena's lap and will be missing the party."

Who would have thought a reputed rogue like Adan would have such a soft spot for children? Not Maysa. She only wished Rafiq shared in his brother's enthusiasm. As far as she knew, he had never held his niece and nephew, and she wondered if he would ever recover from losing the child he'd believed to be his for months. Then as if by magic on this magical night, Cala reached for Rafiq.

Everyone went silent while Maysa held her breath as she awaited her husband's reaction. He hesitated a moment before he took the baby from Adan. Cala extracted her thumb, touched her uncle's face, then laid her head on his shoulder, as if she sensed he needed help with his healing. The scene was so very, very sweet, Maysa's already full heart filled with more joy.

"She apparently realizes who to go to when she needs her demands met," Adan said, shattering the silence. "I hate to disappoint you, Cala, but he will make you jump through hoops before he'll grant you your wish. But if you learn to curtsy—"

"She will not do any such thing," Madison chimed in. "Bow maybe, but never curtsy."

Rafiq tenderly kissed the now sleeping Cala's cheek before returning her to her father. "It is time for us to go now."

Maysa was more than excited to get on with the honeymoon and get out of her heels. "Good night, everyone, and thank you all so much for being there for us."

After doling out hugs and kisses, Maysa and Rafiq entered the armored limousine flanked by escorts on motorcycles. Adan took another car, leaving them alone at last.

Maysa rested her head on Rafiq's shoulder and sighed. "Today is perfect."

He lifted her chin and kissed her softly. "You are perfect."

He might not think so as soon as she asked the question she'd wanted to ask for some time. "Rafiq, do you want to have children?"

"At one time I was not certain I did, but now I am sure I do want children. Perhaps as many as five."

"You cannot be serious, Rafiq. We're both four years past thirty. We wouldn't have time to—"

He touched a fingertip to her lips to silence her. "I am not serious, but I would like to have two. I would also prefer to wait a year before we begin the process, but as Zain said, we may practice frequently until that time."

"I wholeheartedly agree with practicing often and waiting a year, but not any longer. We do need time together before we start a family."

"Fortunately, time is now on our side."

Thankfully, that was true. "There is something else we need to cover. Actually, a few rules."

"So we are back to rules again, are we?"

"A few minor rules. First, I believe it's all right to go to bed angry, as long as we make up in that bed before morning."

"You will receive no argument from me."

"Second, we both need autonomy and time away from each other now and then. We will appreciate each other more when we are together."

From the sour look on his face, evidently that rule did not set well with the king. "How much time?"

She tapped her chin and pretended to think. "I would say perhaps the occasional lunch hour, but never breakfast or dinner. We might want to shower separately—"

"I draw the line there."

She was not surprised by the command. "All right. I wasn't particularly fond of the idea anyway."

He gave her his smile and took her breath in exchange. "Anything else, my queen?"

"I prefer Dr. Queen, remember?"

He lifted her hand and laced their fingers together. "I prefer to call you the woman who saved me from a lonely life. The center of my existence. The love of my life."

The vows were less rushed and more poignant than those they'd exchanged earlier. Beautiful vows coming from an equally beautiful man. "And you, Rafiq Mehdi, have always been, and always will be, the king of my heart."

He touched her face with reverence, then said the words she would never tire of hearing. "*Ana bahebik.* Always."

She laid her hand on his palm, and entrusted him with the rest of her life. "*Ana bahebak.* Forever."

Dr. Maysa Barad-Mehdi had received several miracles at last—permanently reuniting with the man she had wanted most of her life, a career that continually fulfilled her and, most important, realizing that abiding love could be more than enough.

* * * * *

#2245 CANYON
The Westmorelands
Brenda Jackson
When Canyon Westmoreland's ex-lover returns to town, child in tow and needing a safe haven, he's ready to protect what's his, including the son he didn't know he had.

#2246 DEEP IN A TEXAN'S HEART
Texas Cattleman's Club: The Missing Mogul
Sara Orwig
When tradition-bound Texas millionaire Sam Gordon discovers the sexy set designer he shared a passionate night with is pregnant, he proposes. But Lila Hacket won't settle for anything but the real deal—it's true love or bust!

#2247 THE BABY DEAL
Billionaires and Babies
Kat Cantrell
A baby can't be harder than rocket science! But when aerospace billionaire Michael Shaylen inherits a child, he realizes he needs expert help—from the woman who once broke his heart.

#2248 WRONG MAN, RIGHT KISS
Red Garnier
Molly Devaney has been forbidden to Julian Gage his entire life. But when she asks him to help her seduce his brother, Julian must convince her *he's* the man she really wants.

#2249 HIS INSTANT HEIR
Baby Business
Katherine Garbera
When the man who fathered her secret baby comes back to town with plans to take over her family's business, Cari Chandler is suitably shell-shocked. What's a girl to do—especially if the man is irresistible?

#2250 HIS BY DESIGN
Dani Wade
Wedding white meets wedding night when a repressed executive assistant at a design firm finds herself drawn to the unconventional ideas and desires of her new boss.

You can find more information on upcoming Harlequin® titles, free excerpts and more at www.Harlequin.com.

HDCNM0713

REQUEST YOUR FREE BOOKS!
2 FREE NOVELS PLUS 2 FREE GIFTS!

⊕ HARLEQUIN®

Desire

ALWAYS POWERFUL, PASSIONATE AND PROVOCATIVE

YES! Please send me 2 FREE Harlequin Desire® novels and my 2 FREE gifts (gifts are worth about $10). After receiving them, if I don't wish to receive any more books, I can return the shipping statement marked "cancel." If I don't cancel, I will receive 6 brand-new novels every month and be billed just $4.55 per book in the U.S. or $4.99 per book in Canada. That's a savings of at least 13% off the cover price! It's quite a bargain! Shipping and handling is just 50¢ per book in the U.S. and 75¢ per book in Canada.* I understand that accepting the 2 free books and gifts places me under no obligation to buy anything. I can always return a shipment and cancel at any time. Even if I never buy another book, the two free books and gifts are mine to keep forever.

225/326 HDN F4ZC

Name	(PLEASE PRINT)	
Address		Apt. #
City	State/Prov.	Zip/Postal Code

Signature (if under 18, a parent or guardian must sign)

Mail to the Harlequin® Reader Service:
IN U.S.A.: P.O. Box 1867, Buffalo, NY 14240-1867
IN CANADA: P.O. Box 609, Fort Erie, Ontario L2A 5X3

**Want to try two free books from another line?
Call 1-800-873-8635 or visit www.ReaderService.com.**

* Terms and prices subject to change without notice. Prices do not include applicable taxes. Sales tax applicable in N.Y. Canadian residents will be charged applicable taxes. Offer not valid in Quebec. This offer is limited to one order per household. Not valid for current subscribers to Harlequin Desire books. All orders subject to credit approval. Credit or debit balances in a customer's account(s) may be offset by any other outstanding balance owed by or to the customer. Please allow 4 to 6 weeks for delivery. Offer available while quantities last.

HD13R

SPECIAL EXCERPT FROM

Desire

*Canyon Westmoreland is about to get the
surprise of his life!
Don't miss a moment of the drama in
CANYON
by* New York Times *and* USA TODAY *bestselling author
Brenda Jackson
Available August 2013
only from Harlequin® Desire®!*

Canyon watched Keisha turn into Mary's Little Lamb Day Care. He frowned. Why would she be stopping at a day care? Maybe she had volunteered to babysit for someone tonight.

He slid into a parking spot and watched as she got out of her car and went inside, smiling. Hopefully, her good mood would continue when she saw that he'd followed her. His focus stayed on her, concentrating on the sway of her hips with every step she took, until she was no longer in sight. A few minutes later she walked out of the building, smiling and chatting with the little boy whose hand she was holding—a boy who was probably around two years old.

Canyon studied the little boy's features. The kid could be a double for Denver, Canyon's three-year-old nephew. An uneasy feeling stirred his insides. Then, as he studied the little boy, Canyon took in a gasping breath. There was only one reason the little boy looked so much like a Westmoreland.

Canyon gripped the steering wheel, certain steam was coming out of his ears.

He didn't remember easing his seat back, unbuckling his

seat belt or opening the car door. Neither did he remember walking toward Keisha. However, he would always remember the look on her face when she saw him. What he saw on her features was surprise, guilt and remorse.

As he got closer, defensiveness followed by fierce protectiveness replaced those other emotions. She pulled her son—the child he was certain was *their* son—closer to her side. "What are you doing here, Canyon?"

He came to a stop in front of her. His body was radiating anger from the inside out. His gaze left her face to look down at the little boy, who was clutching the hem of Keisha's skirt and staring up at him with distrustful eyes.

Canyon shifted his gaze back up to meet Keisha's eyes. In a voice shaking with fury, he asked, "Would you like to tell me why I didn't know I had a son?"

CANYON
by New York Times *and* USA TODAY *bestselling author*
Brenda Jackson
Available August 2013
only from Harlequin® Desire®!

HARLEQUIN®

A *Romance* FOR EVERY MOOD™

Love the Harlequin book you just read?

Your opinion matters.

Review this book on your favorite book site, review site, blog or your own social media properties and share your opinion with other readers!